Seven Range Shifters

Cowboy Wolf Trouble

Cowboy in Wolf's Clothing

Wicked Cowboy Wolf

Fierce Cowboy Wolf

Wild Cowboy Wolf

Cowboy Wolf Outlaw

Cowboy Wolf Christmas

The Rogue Brotherhood

Shadow Hunter

Rogue Wolf Hunter

THE VAMPIRE'S
HUNTER

KAIT BALLENGER

KB

To my readers,
for following me through one world
and into the next

We want readers to be well-informed.
If you would like to know if this book has any elements of concern
for you, please check the author's website for details:
www.kaitballenger.com

1

———

Dani Harper wasn't certain how she'd found herself here, and yet...here she was. She stood frozen inside The Diner King, eyes locked on the familiar cowboy who made his way toward her with unwavering intent. Shit, this was unexpected, but she shouldn't have been surprised.

She felt that way about a lot of things in her life—as if she'd somehow ended up there without intention or plan. But this time, watching her estranged brother waltz into the diner where she worked with all the prowl of one of the preternatural creatures he famously hunted, the feeling was harder to ignore.

"Goddamn it!" a sharp, aging voice bellowed to her right. "You flighty, dimwitted—"

Dani blinked, instantly wrenched back into the moment. To the sticky, fry-oil rent air of the diner. To the old bank pen and notepad tucked into the cornflower apron that squeezed her waist, and to the steaming, now overflowing ceramic mug spilling coffee onto the table in front of Mr. Dougherty.

A clearly pissed-off, *human* Mr. Dougherty.

"Shit." She scrambled to right the coffee pot in her hand.

She was supposed to be taking Mr. Dougherty's order, not speculating on whatever kind of supernatural trouble her brother's unexpected arrival meant. Which since Mr. Dougherty was a regular—a very *human* regular, just like every other lost soul here—meant a boring coffee with two sugars, one cream, and then fetching his biscuits and gravy as fast as the kitchen could cook it, all before he yelled at her for being "slow" again.

Never mind that she usually served up orders faster than any other waitress on the midnight scheduling block and with a more genuine smile to boot. Escaping Mr. Dougherty's ire was its own kind of skill, and from the moment she'd overpoured his coffee that ship had sailed faster than the menu's fish and chips could send a person sailing to the restroom—which was undeniably and disgustingly fast.

Mr. Dougherty grumbled at her, the jowls of his cheeks wiggling in anger. "Why, you—"

"I'm so sorry, Mr. Dougherty. Let me grab a towel," she muttered quickly, before she scurried away from the table.

Depositing the coffee pot onto the hot plate, Dani snatched a spare bussing rag from the sink and grabbed a replacement saucer from the dish rack, prepared to head back to Mr. Dougherty, but a soft hand quickly stayed her arm.

"Isn't that your brother?" Thelma piled three steaming orders of hashbrowns with a side of bacon onto one arm, before plopping a plated coney island covered in sloppy chili onto the other. She nodded to where Quinn now sat on the far side of the diner. Meanwhile, the smell of fried potato and chili invaded Dani's nose.

Her brother was watching them, waiting for her. Because of course he was.

Dani's nerves shot into overdrive.

"What?" she blinked at Thelma, still dazed from the Mr. Dougherty incident.

"I said, isn't that your brother?" Thelma nodded toward the shadowed face beneath the Stetson.

Brow furrowed, Dani's eyes shot between where her brother sat, and the veteran waitress who waited for her answer. Thelma didn't exactly look like the type to know about shifters, vamps, and witches—the world's supernatural underbelly. Most humans didn't. But what did Dani know? She supposed someone could likely say the same of her.

Lifting a brow, Dani lowered her voice. "How did you—?"

Thelma smiled, batting Dani's arm playfully, completely unaware of Dani's insinuation. "You showed me an old picture of him once, remember?"

Dani blinked. Right. Thelma recognized Quinn for who he was to her, not the role he played. The role everyone else of any paranormal importance in her life knew her brother for. Figured. It was yet another sobering reminder that here in this small little town where she'd landed herself, she was alone in more ways than one. Burdened with a knowledge Thelma and her coworkers would never endure.

And yet...strangely nostalgic for the absence of everything she'd left behind.

"Yeah, I...I suppose I did, didn't I?" She smiled weakly.

Thelma shook her head. "Well, what are you waiting for, sugar? You going to make him wait in that booth all day or are you going to go see him?"

Dani glanced toward where Mr. Dougherty was now cursing.

"Don't you worry about that old curmudgeon." Thelma nodded toward the regular. "I'll take care of him." She gave Dani a supportive wink as she gently tugged the wet rag away from her, somehow still managing to balance all her plates and trays.

"I suppose you're right." Dani nodded, wringing her hands. Clearly, she couldn't avoid her brother forever. Even if she wanted to.

Slowly, she made her way over to the booth.

"Quinn," she mumbled shyly.

"Dani." Her brother's voice was as gruff and hardened as she remembered. Pure cowboy.

No hint of the city slicker he could have been. He stood and pulled her into a brief hug.

"It's been a while," Dani said lamely, wiping her hands down the front of her apron.

For a moment, Quinn didn't bother to say anything, just tilted that hat of his in acknowledgement.

An awkward silence passed between them. Tense and heavy. Full of all the things neither of them wanted to say.

"Why didn't you come see me at the bar?" Dani asked, attempting to fill the quiet, though the constant clatter of forks against dishes, the sizzle of the diner's griddle and Thelma's usual hollering about why her other orders weren't up yet sort of did the trick.

Quinn frowned. "I hear having a hunter around isn't good for business," he said, his mouth pressing into a thin line.

Dani nodded, tentatively sliding into the booth across from him.

It felt...strange sitting there with him, like when they were young and she'd adored him.

"I suppose Trixie told you to back off then?"

Quinn's Stetson dipped low on his brow. "In not so kind of words."

That sounded like Trixie alright—the bartending witch served as the proprietress and owner of the newest incarnation of the Midnight Coyote, a supernatural-only bar that'd recently relocated not too far outside Detroit. About an hour drive from middle-of-nowhere here.

On occasion when they were short-staffed, Dani sometimes worked there on the weekends, which meant she knew firsthand the magic-wielding bartendress was a force to reckoned with. Hell, Dani owed her life to Trixie, along with her partner, Malcolm. It hadn't been that long ago that the other woman had saved her when she'd been unable to save herself, hands down, no questions asked. Dani could never be that strong willed, as much as she admired it. As much as she considered Trixie a friend.

"So, what brings you here then?" Dani forced a smile.

Quinn gave her an incredulous look. "I could ask you the same thing."

Thelma showed up at their table a moment later, quickly setting down two mugs of steaming coffee, before Dani was forced to introduce Quinn. Thankfully, her brother was unusually polite to Thelma, accommodating the woman's need for friendly small talk, until Thelma left them alone again.

Quinn turned his attention back toward her. "So, you've switched from vamps to witches, huh?"

Dani clutched the mug her coworker had given her like a lifeline. "Trixie's been good to me. She's...helped me out when I needed it."

Unlike you.

She'd never dare say such a hurtful thing, but that didn't stop her from thinking it.

Still, the unspoken words seemed to settle between them, heavy and present.

She couldn't exactly blame her brother for not coming to her rescue. Lord knew they'd chosen different paths. He'd long ago become a renowned hunter for an elite clandestine organization of humans—the Execution Underground—the only protective force that stood between the predators of the supernatural world and humanity. And her, well...she drifted wherever the wind blew her, which was often into the arms of the wrong man, or vampire as it were, more than her elder brother would ever care for.

She was a wistful human nobody in a sea of powerful beings, as she'd been reminded more than once before, and Quinn wasn't about to let her forget it.

"I heard you got yourself into some real trouble back in Billings," Quinn said, cutting straight to the elephant in the room.

So, he'd heard.

Dani felt her ears turn red.

Of course, he'd heard. Him and everyone else under the sun. It was why she was here in this damn diner, after all. Apparently, it wasn't enough to be made a fool of, to become a powerful vampire's human plaything, drugged and taken advantage of like she was a pathetic human toy, but now everyone had to know about it. Her hurt, her shame. The supernatural community wasn't large, and she stood out as one of the few humans in it.

"Yeah, well, that's over now, isn't it?" She forced another smile.

And I'm fine, thanks for asking. Not that anyone ever did.

"Is it?" Quinn lifted a brow.

Unshed tears prickled her eyes. This is exactly why she had no desire to talk to Quinn. Her brother had never approved of her life choices, even the ones she couldn't control, which was why they hardly ever spoke. She couldn't handle his constant judgement, so she'd just sort of...drifted away. Like she did with a lot of things. But that's what happened when you came from a broken family, wasn't it?

"Why are you here, Quinn?" she sighed.

Quinn leaned back in the booth, propping his arms over the cracked vinyl seat. "Can't a man check up on his baby sister without getting the third degree?"

She lowered her eyes, instantly ashamed. Her brother had never been unkind to her, even if she didn't care for his protective instincts. "I'm sorry. It's just...I...wasn't expecting you. That's all."

When she glanced back, Quinn's gaze seemed to have softened then. However, briefly. Like how he'd looked at her when they'd been children. Before she'd been a disappointment to him. Back when it'd been them against the world, and before he'd stopped fighting her battles for her.

"How are you, Dani? Really?"

She gave a little shrug. "Good as I'll ever be."

Quinn didn't respond.

Dani shook her head. "You know how it is. I've got a job now. Two, actually. Though I'm getting fewer hours at the bar these days, but I'm making my own rent, barely. Waitressing gives me enough to keep food on the table, and you know, that's about all I could ask for really."

Quinn grunted his disagreement. "And why here?" He gestured to the diner around them. To all the humans in it.

Like them and yet, somehow, different. Neither of them would ever be one among them.

Not with the knowledge they'd been forced to carry since she'd been barely more than girl, and Quinn barely a man.

Back then, her brother had been her anchor, though he'd been just as orphaned as she'd been, thrust into a knowledge of a supernatural world neither of them had ever wanted a part of.

Now, things were different.

For a moment, Dani wasn't certain how to answer.

How *had* she ended up here?

However, it'd happened, it was better than before, that's for certain. Better than when she'd been trapped under Cillian's thumb, unable to escape, and yet...

"Trixie thought it'd be better if I stepped away from the community for a bit," she said, lowering her voice. As if speaking in whispers could somehow hide her shame.

"*Trixie* thought it'd be better?" Quinn lifted a brow as if to say, *But not you?*

Dani winced. That was the thing about her brother, he'd always seen straight to the heart of her. She'd once liked that. When exactly had he started judging her for it?

"We both decided, I guess?" She shrugged a shoulder.

Quinn didn't appear convinced.

Dani huffed again. "Did you come here to just point out all the ways I've disappointed you, Quinn, or are you here for a reason?"

Quinn's eyes widened, like he was surprised at how uncharacteristically confrontational she was being. "I don't think you're a disappointment, Dani. I just think you deserve better. I wish *you* thought you deserved better, that's all."

And there it was.

Dani couldn't help it. She was crying now. No longer able to hold back her tears.

She swiped at them with the back of her hand, but there was no stop to it. The floodgates had opened. "And you came here just to tell me that?" She sniffled.

"No." Quinn shook his head.

The tears came faster then, silent but steady.

Of course she'd known that. She'd known from the moment he'd walked into the diner that she wasn't the reason he was here, and yet, she'd still allowed herself to believe otherwise, to hope that someone was finally here to save her, to give her the home base she'd been searching for since long before either of them had ever been orphaned. Their parents had never exactly been kind before their deaths, but still, she'd been dumb enough to trust Quinn when he said he was here to check up on her.

That had always been her problem, hadn't it? She was too trusting. Too naïve. Everyone said so. She'd *let* herself be taken advantage of time and time again.

But where was that same ire for those who'd taken advantage of her, for those who'd hurt her? For all the men, the vampires and otherwise who'd made a fool of her all because she had a kind heart that they'd found easy to exploit? Where was the distaste for *them*?

Quinn shifted uncomfortably in his seat, unused to her tears. "We need your help."

"We," she repeated knowingly, having to suppress a gurgling, unamused laugh.

"The Execution Underground," Quinn elaborated.

She knew exactly who "we" meant, but her brother answered as if she'd asked a question. No surprise there. She knew without a doubt everyone believed she wasn't smart.

Naïve. Flighty. Dimwitted. Just like Mr. Dougherty had said. Men were always talking down to her. Hell, women too. Always assuming she didn't know. And why bother to correct them?

There was little point to it.

She'd lost that fight long ago, before it'd ever really started.

People saw a pretty face, a kind heart, and a forgiving nature wrapped up in a scared, damaged soul and they made assumptions. They always did. She was both Madonna and whore.

"What could the Execution Underground possibly want with me?"

Quinn reached inside his jacket and pulled out a photo, sliding it across the table toward her.

For a beat, Dani simply stared at the blank backing, until finally she couldn't stop herself from flipping it over and examining the handsome silhouette beneath. Immediately, her heart plunged to her feet, taking her stomach along with it. No.

No, no, no, no. *Anyone* but him.

"What do you want with him?" she heard herself whisper before she'd even fully registered the question.

Quinn lifted an impatient brow, pointing to the photo of the devilishly handsome vampire. "You know as well as I do Corbin's involved with the *Cosa della notte* syndicate."

Dani shook her head, refusing to answer. "I don't have anything to say to you about that."

The *Cosa della notte* was the vampire equivalent of the human mafia. Its members ruthless. The worst of which treated humans like her as if they were little more than cattle.

And yes, she knew without a doubt that Corbin was involved in it, though he'd never been anything but dazzlingly kind to her. Cillian had been too, though, before Trixie and Malcolm had saved her from him, from herself, and from the abuse she'd gotten herself tangled into.

They'd left the ancient bloodsucker for dead on the floor of Corbin's club.

No, Corbin Blackwell, the Blood Rose's owner, a charming British vampire who was entirely too much of a smooth talker that he *always* got his way, may have broken her heart years ago without even knowing it, but that didn't mean she was going to rat him out. Not like this. From what Trixie had told her, Corbin had played a key part in getting her away from Cillian, in ending the abusive relationship she'd been stuck in, and for that, she'd be forever grateful to him.

No matter how much the sight of him made her chest ache.

Unwillingly, her hand flitted to the pocket of her apron, to the skeleton key she kept on a necklace chain hidden under her clothes. A reminder that she was stronger than she believed herself to be.

Like how she'd once thought she could feel whenever Corbin had captured her with that all too entrancing gaze, though she knew better now. The ancient British vampire would never be so sentimental as to gift anything of meaning to her. She wasn't that important to him, even if he'd been kind to her now and again. She was just someone worthy of his pity, that's all.

Before Dani knew what was happening, her brother was talking again, lobbing words at her that when strung together in her mind didn't make any sense—words like duty, and bravery, and justice—things she'd only ever experienced on T.V. or in the overpowering shadow of her brother's presence.

"We believe he may have insight into Lucien's whereabouts."

Immediately, Dani's blood ran cold. Vague drug-hazed memories of harsh hands and even sharper fangs assaulted her, holding her down. It hadn't been enough for Cillian to hurt her again and again, but then he'd been certain to share her with his fucked-up friends, though not Corbin, of course. He hadn't been among them.

Dani was trembling before she'd even realized the memory had overtaken her.

Quinn reached out and touched her hand, bringing her back to herself and causing her to nearly jump out of her skin.

Her brother's gaze softened then, and this time, it stayed that way.

Which somehow only made it worse.

"We need someone who will blend in. Someone whose been a part of that world and—"

"And everyone knows I'm nothing more than a fanger whore," she finished for him.

Quinn's shoulders stiffened, making him look unexpectedly tense, and to her surprise, ashamed. He chose his next words carefully. "I was going to say everyone knows that you've been *involved* with vampires in the syndicate before."

"Same thing, just prettier words." She swiped at her tears again.

Quinn sighed, clearly recognizing this was a battle he wouldn't win. "I know you think I'm here for them, but Dani," he gripped her hand, "I wouldn't have come if I didn't believe you could do this. If I didn't think that you might want—"

"Revenge?" she finished.

"Yes," Quinn answered, more confident than she'd given

him credit for. "To make sure this doesn't happen to anyone else again."

The prick of his words was like a knife to the heart.

"That's not my responsibility," she breathed.

Quinn nodded. "You're right. It isn't."

And yet...

Here he was. Asking it of her anyway.

Because for once, in some small way, her brother believed she could be like him.

That she could be brave. That she could fight for someone else, if not for herself.

Dani let out a small shivering sigh of resignation. She'd known whatever Quinn was here to ask her to do, she would agree. It didn't matter if that was what she really wanted or not, because that was what Dani always did.

She endured, and thus, she survived. Wherever the wind blew her.

And this time, it was leading her straight into the arms of a vampire who'd no doubt break her heart.

"What do I need to do?"

2

The neon red lights were a nice touch, if a bit, expected.

Corbin Blackwell surveyed the club he owned with a distant disinterest, his phone buzzing in his pocket for the umpteenth time that evening. The music which beat through The Blood Rose's speakers was incessant, the sound punctuated only by the clink of amber lit glasses and the occasional shout of laughter from the sweat-covered crowd below. To his right, the club's designer droned on about the latest update and renovation, her voice blending in with the din as Corbin's phone buzzed once more.

He let out a harsh sigh. "If you'll excuse me..."

Brow pinched, Corbin pulled the infernal device from his pocket, reading the array of messages flashing across the screen.

CASSANDRA: Where *are* you?

Cassandra: I said I was sorry.

Cassandra: Corbin, pleeeease. *pouty face*

Cassandra: I promise I'll be nicer next time, if you get me that dress I want. *heart eyes*

Cassandra: Corbin?

Cassandra: Corbin??

Cassandra: CORBIN?!?! *angry face*

Cassandra: Fine. If you're going to be an asshole, then forget it...

CORBIN SWALLOWED down a thinly veiled sneer. As far as he was concerned, there was only one asshole in this situation, and for once, it wasn't him.

Huffing, he quickly pocketed his phone again.

"Sir?" The interior designer to his left probed, drawing his attention once more.

She was a heavy-set lesbian artist with a flair for fashion and color. Not uninteresting for a human, if a bit droll.

Corbin lifted a brow. "Pardon?"

"I said, are the lights not to your liking?" she repeated.

Of course. Professional as ever. All his people were.

Even if he was feeling far from it.

Corbin drew another sip of his whiskey, scanning over the club once more as he contemplated the question at hand. Tonight, the atmosphere inside The Blood Rose's Chicago location was hot and stuffy, filled to the brim with one-too-many sweaty bodies, though not enough to break fire codes, but the red neon lights *did* add a subtle erotic touch.

"The lights are lovely. Thank you," he said, flashing a charming smile he didn't at all feel, though one he knew, no doubt, would appease.

"Don't mind him, Alex. He just has blue balls, because

he's dumped his latest plaything, that's all." A large hand suddenly clapped him on the shoulder.

Corbin scowled, his eyes darting to Kharis, his so-called friend. "Can we *please* not talk about my balls in polite company, *or* Cassandra for that matter?" He turned to the designer once more. "That'll be all for now, Alex. Thank you."

The designer nodded, accepting her cue to leave.

Once they were alone, Kharis shot him an incredulous look. "Why come in tonight, if all you're going to do is sulk?"

"Does it look like I'm sulking?" Corbin lifted a brow, before he turned back toward the dance floor, watching the controlled chaos on the level below. A new song had come on, some electronic beat or another that the humans inside the club went wild for.

Kharis waved a hand in dismissal. "You're always sulking these days. Normally, you drink me under the table."

Corbin lifted his glass of whisky to his lips, the amber catching like fire in the light of the club's crimson glow. "Normally, I don't have plans in the morning." He took another generous sip. "And I'm not sulking. I'm *working*. You should try it sometime."

Kharis frowned, clearly unconvinced. "Is this really all over that bloody siren then?"

Corbin didn't bother to look at the other vampire, rubbing his brow, before he took another sip. "For what it's worth, Cassandra was a mutual decision." Not that his sex life was anyone else's business. Underboss or otherwise.

"In other words, you got bored with her?" Kharis let out a harsh bark of a laugh, easily distinguishable despite the thumping music.

The ancient Greek knew him all too well.

A round of shrieks sounded from a drunken bachelorette party, shrill and raucous.

"Wouldn't you?" An unamused smirk crossed Corbin's lips.

Cassandra had been fun while she lasted, but while sex with the fiery siren had been... adequate, her constant demands that he drape her in finery like she was his mistress had quickly become tedious. Sirens were greedy, tiresome things. Hungry for adulation and little more.

He should have learned his lesson from Odysseus.

Still chuckling his amusement, Kharis joined him overlooking the balcony of the club's second floor. The human bachelorette was throwing back a neon green shot now, swaying.

"All I'm saying is, for a man about to have everything he wants, you seem awfully melancholy."

Corbin shrugged, swirling his drink. "I find myself increasingly bored these days," he admitted.

Kharis let out an undignified snort. "Of course, you do. You're about to lose your favorite pastime."

"Which is?" Corbin grumbled.

Kharis only shook his head at him. "Revenge is supposed to taste sweet, my friend."

Corbin scoffed. "Revenge is a poison no sane man would drink, and yet, here we are."

"No one ever dared call you sane, old boy." Corbin felt more than saw Kharis hesitate, before the other vampire lifted one full, dark brow. "You're not getting cold feet, are you?"

Corbin cut him a biting look.

Kharis lifted his hands in surrender, clearly recognizing he'd pushed too far. "I'm only trying to help, that's all."

"My feet are not cold," Corbin said, punctuating each

word with his lack of amusement as he watched the bar below. One of the club's many bartenders was lighting a line of pink martini drinks aflame. "No colder than your bed each night," he mumbled.

"Now I know you're sulking! It's the only time you bother to insult me," Kharis protested.

His friend fell silent for a moment as he took a sip of his drink, lowering his voice though they were already alone. Some discussions were only meant for whispers.

"And the distraction you need to keep Lucien busy? Have you found it yet?"

Corbin didn't deign to answer.

Kharis may have been his friend, but he wouldn't be managed.

"Fuck, Corbin," Kharis swore, his face growing suddenly serious. "You know you can't dazzle your way out of this one?"

"You should know better than anyone that I can *dazzle* my way out of anything." Corbin cast his friend a sidelong glance. "And I'm working on it."

Kharis scoffed. "In other words, we're fucked."

"I said, I'm working on it."

"Well, work faster."

This time, Corbin didn't hide the scowl that pulled at his lips. "If you came here simply to nag me, Kharis, then why don't you—"

Without warning, a shout sounded from the far side of the club below, drawing Kharis' attention. His friend's gaze shot to the downstairs floor, before he let out a low wolf whistle, instantly enthralled. "Well, well, well, would you look what the cat dragged in."

Unamused, Corbin followed Kharis' gaze to scuffle below, something the club's bouncers would no doubt take care of, though from the amused way Kharis' smile lit, his friend appeared as if he were a cat who'd been gifted a rather large blow of cream.

"I believe your night just got far more interesting." Kharis smirked.

Corbin's gaze fell to the scene before him, his eyes quickly locking onto Kharis' target and staying there for a moment more. In an instant, a low growl rumbled in his throat, his fangs aching. He swallowed down a curse.

What the fuck was Dani doing here?

He scanned the human woman near his dance floor from head to toe. The black dress. The lean legs. The subtle curved form. Tonight, the gold undertones in her blond hair pulsed red beneath the club's crimson glow. Instantly, Corbin's cock stiffened.

To say Dani Harper was beautiful was an understatement.

She was the kind of ethereal beauty that every man wanted to know, to possess, to own, because what man, what vampire, could resist a woman who was so beautiful, so doe-eyed and innocent that she might as well be a lamb brought to slaughter? Who among them didn't desire to take that kind of womanly innocence and claim it as his own? To twist and corrupt it?

It was in their fucking natures.

A woman like Dani aroused the predator in all of them.

Him more than most.

His eyes fell to the vampire across from her, the one clutching her hand as she fruitlessly attempted to pull away. Obviously, the message he'd given her to get gone and stay gone hadn't been clear enough when he'd saved her once before. When he'd had to painstakingly extract her from

Cillian's clutches, putting his own neck, his own goals at risk.

If there was one thing Dani was reliable for it was waltzing into the most dangerous of situations with little more than a tender-hearted smile on her face, floating through life, as if she were waiting for him to swoop in and save her as he had dozens of times before.

The woman lived to find trouble.

And yet...

Somehow, he always found her.

What exactly did that say for his character?

"It looks like someone's no longer waiting around in hopes for you, old boy."

"Shut up, Kharis." Corbin was already moving, his eyes falling to Zane, the vampire who attempted to pull her close, despite Dani's resistance.

Every bloodsucker in the room was eyeing her.

Forget sirens. Dani's blood called to them, more than most.

"I think I may have just found my distraction," Corbin muttered over his shoulder as he descended the second-floor stairs, his eyes flashing red and not from the club lights above.

Behind him, Kharis laughed. "With that look, I'm not confident you won't drain her yourself before morning."

Corbin was already half-way across the club toward her, before he grumbled in answer, "You and me both."

3

Dani had been in Chicago all of five minutes and already she found herself in trouble.

"Come on, sweetheart. Smile that pretty grin again."

She tugged against the vampire who held a near death-grip on her wrist, fighting but failing to slip away. "I really need to—"

"I'll take it from here, Zane," a smooth voice from behind cut Dani's words short, sending an all too familiar shiver down her spine.

A large hand slipped to the front of her throat, another gripping her elbow as its owner pulled her deliciously close, causing Zane's hand to fall away.

It was a possessive embrace. The kind that signaled to anyone and everyone near, Zane included, that she was more than a pretty face, she was an object to be claimed, and claimed she'd been. Dani didn't need to see who held her to recognize the vampire those lithe hands belonged to. Her body was already aware of him. It always had been.

"Corbin," she breathed, melting into his warmth a little too readily.

That was one thing the movies never got right—the idea that a vampire's touch was cold. Corbin had been the first to show her that with little more than a brush of his hand. She'd been young, foolish then, and she'd wanted him from the moment she'd met him nearly ten years ago.

Old habits died hard, she supposed.

The warmth of his breath brushed against her ear, causing a relieved sigh to tear from her lips. "What an unexpected surprise, my love."

My love?

Dani's eyes widened, even as she felt her nipples grow stiff.

In all the years she'd known Corbin, despite all the flirting, toying, and teasing, he'd never once claimed her as his own. Never touched, caressed, or kissed her. Had never done anything more than tantalize and provoke, exactly what he did with *everyone*. As if she were forbidden. Or at least, as if he had only a cursory interest in her. Nothing more.

And he'd certainly never told her he loved her. Though foolishly she'd nearly come close to confessing as much to him once upon a decade ago, but ages had passed since then. She knew better now. Not to mention, it'd been nearly a year or longer since she'd last seen him, and even before Cillian's death, whole seasons had often passed between when she and Corbin spoke, but he was speaking now, his accent crisp and close.

"Thank you for keeping an eye on her, Zane. She does love to get herself into trouble, don't you, darling?" Corbin's grip on her neck tightened, promising to play somewhere between pleasure and pain as he leaned in. "Play along," he hissed into her ear.

Dani nodded in agreement.

Anything to get her away from Zane.

Corbin held her flush against him now, her bottom pressing against the fly of his suit enough that she could feel the hardened length of his cock beneath. Dani bit her lower lip. She didn't need any acting skills to fake the eager groan that escaped her as Corbin's lips brushed over her throat, one of his fangs tracing the fluttering beat of her pulse.

She whimpered a little, arching against him like she wanted—no, *needed*—more. Heat slickened between her legs. Good Lord, she wanted him. She always had, she supposed. She'd known that when she'd come here, that she'd never truly managed to get over him.

But what in God's name was he playing at?

"You mean to tell me she's yours?" Zane said, fleetingly drawing both her and Corbin's attention toward him once more.

Like Corbin, Zane was long and lean, the planes of his clothes belied with a subtle, yet impressive form, though Dani knew firsthand a vampire's true strength didn't lie in their muscles. She'd learned that the hard way with Cillian, then Lucien. A vampire's looks could be deceiving, and while Zane was the kind of vampire who perhaps would have impressed her before, she wasn't that person anymore. Not after all she'd been through, and certainly not now that she'd started to understand why she'd always ended up in the arms of the wrong man.

Because the only vampire she'd ever *truly* wanted had never wanted her in return.

The same vampire whose lips were currently trailing their way over her throat, like he couldn't just smell her desire, he could taste it on her skin. This situation between them was supposed to be fake, except...

Was it possible to orgasm from a vampire's kiss alone?

Because Corbin hadn't even bitten her, and already she felt close.

"Don't be a fool, Zane. Of course, she's mine," Corbin's grip on her neck loosened, turning into a caress. "Unequivocally." He spoke right into her ear, his words both familiar and foreign.

Good Lord, she didn't care if it made her basic, his accent had always thrilled her.

"Apologies, Corbin," Zane said, immediately casting his eyes low.

If there'd been any doubt about who was in charge here, Corbin crushed it with a single look. Dani didn't need to see the expression on his face to know it'd turned instantly cold. She'd seen that same violence in his eyes, aimed at his enemies, more than once before.

"That'll be all, Zane," Corbin hissed, though his unspoken message was clear.

Touch what's mine, and I'll end you.

A harsh shiver rippled down her spine.

Abruptly, the hand at her throat disappeared, Corbin rotating her to face him and lifting her barely an inch off the floor, just enough to whisk her to the other side of the club with a supernatural speed that stole her breath away. He hadn't given Zane so much as a chance to protest or retaliate. Not that she'd ever expected the other vampire to do so.

Among the *Cosa della notte* fucking with Corbin would have been akin to Zane signing his own death warrant. There were worse crimes, of course, but she didn't want to consider those.

Dani blinked, dazed from how fast they'd moved.

"What are you doing?" she breathed, finally looking up at Corbin, from where he still held her close. Intimately close. As if she did, in fact, belong to him.

"You heard me, Dani. Be a good girl and play along."

They were tucked into a darkened alcove now, pleasantly alone, though the club's patrons were still very much in view. Anyone who wanted to see them could, and she had more than a passing feeling that was what Corbin had chosen it for.

Without warning, Corbin gently pushed her against the wall, pressing her flush against him. This time, they were face-to-face, their mouths unsettlingly close, which meant he could not only hear and feel her, but he could see, could taste every reaction, every breath she took. His hand fell to her throat again, one thumb tracing the beat of her pulse almost reverently. His other made quick work of hooking one of her legs over his hip, before suddenly that same hand dipped beneath her skirt.

Like he planned to touch her, finger her, right there beside the dance floor.

For all his club to see.

Dani's breath caught, her voice going hoarse.

"Corbin, you can't just—" Her eyes darted around the club, to all the patrons that could be watching them.

"What *I* do in *my* club is my business." That dark endless gaze seared through her. "Now, do you want to sell this as real or not, love?"

Real or...

Dani's head struggled to catch up with her body, considering she'd all but stopped thinking the moment he'd first pulled her close. Her eyes traced over Corbin's handsome face. The sharp cheekbones. The sculpted jaw. The chiseled brow and regal nose.

He was harshly beautiful in a way even few vampires were—and that was saying something, considering as an undead species, they were pretty much all freaking beautiful —but Corbin took the word angelic and put it to shame. Especially whenever he flashed that white-toothed roguish grin of his. Ever the charmer. The Devil *had* been an angel once, she supposed...

And this devil clearly meant for her to play along.

To *fake* as if she wanted him.

For all watching eyes to see.

How did he not realize she *wanted* him to hold her close? She'd never have to fake it. Not with him.

"Now, for the sake of my reputation, do try to moan," he whispered, causing her to shiver as his hand dipped beneath her dress to the supple skin of her thigh below. "I promise to keep my hands thoroughly to myself after this."

"Please don't," she whispered.

Whether he thought she was pleading for him to stop or that she was begging him for more, she'd never be certain. All Dani knew then was sensation, feeling.

The sudden press of Corbin's hot mouth at her throat. The brush of hardened fang against the tender skin of her ear. The weight of his muscled body as he settled over her, his shoulders broad and heavy, his hips narrow, and the rough brush of his fingers as he toyed with the laced edge of her panties whilst his lips caressed her. Good Lord, she was in over her head.

Dani bucked her hips forward, nudging against him eagerly in a feeble attempt to guide his hand lower, but still, he didn't touch her. Not where she truly wanted him to.

Because none of this was real, of course.

It was all for show. Meant to turn heads and inspire whispers.

Like everything Corbin did.

But he *could* have touched her there, if he wanted to, if he chose. He could have slipped inside her and taken and taken and taken and still she would have been eager to give more. Hell, if she'd even had so much as half a mind to stop him, there would have been little she could do to resist. If he'd wanted to take advantage, he could have glamoured her into submission. She'd experienced it with Cillian more than once before.

But he didn't.

Instead, Corbin held her close, only touching her above her clothes in ways that benefitted them both, in ways that could easily be forgiven, situation considered. Enough to put on a show to protect her without ever fully crossing the line, out of respect for them both.

And somehow, that only made Dani want him more.

She let out a needy, little keen, something wanton between a whimper and a moan. She hadn't felt this way in months, longer even. She bucked her hips forward again, unexpectedly eager. His hand and his fingers were so close to where she wanted him. So ridiculously close.

And yet...

The space between them may as well have been a chasm for how he dared not cross it.

Not without her permission.

"Please," she begged. "Touch me, Corbin."

At the sound of his name on her lips, Corbin froze. He stayed like that for a long beat, his body utterly still, as if it were a struggle to maintain control, before slowly he pulled back to look at her, staring down from where he'd been lavishing her throat. His dark eyes were ablaze in a way she'd never seen before, a sharp and piercing red, his mouth no more than hairsbreadth away.

So close.

Something violent sparked in his gaze then. Something harsh and crimson and feral.

"You're playing a dangerous game, Dani," he whispered.

Yes, yes, she was, but she'd known that when she'd decided to come here, hadn't she? She was intimately familiar with the threat vampires posed, and yet, she'd came anyway.

She'd never claimed to have much in the way of self-preservation.

Corbin's thumb traced over the lace edge of her under-garments once more, seductive and warm. To the unknowing eye, it appeared as if he were pleasuring her, but it was only an illusion. Not nearly enough to satisfy.

"Please," she whispered again, unable to say anything more.

She was too caught up in her own need, her own desire for him.

The Adam's apple at Corbin's throat bobbed as he swallowed, his gaze surprisingly soft. "You don't know what you're asking of me, Dani," he whispered to her.

"No, I don't." Feeling more than a little brazen, Dani gripped the lapels of his suit coat. "But...I... I think you want this too."

Corbin chuckled, the sound dark and a little morose. "Oh, you *are* far more dangerous than anyone gives you credit for, aren't you, darling?" He cupped her chin in his hand then, the edge of his thumb tracing over her lips, smearing her red lipstick.

For a moment, a dark, greedy sort of hunger flashed in his eyes, a look of longing so deep she wasn't certain it could be satisfied, before it quickly disappeared, replaced instead with a thin veneer of amusement, as if he took immense pleasure in being the one who'd smudged her makeup, who'd sullied her mouth.

Corbin's gaze dipped low, raking over the flush in her cheeks, her hardened nipples, all the ways she responded to him, and for a moment, she was certain he'd deny her again.

He had every other time before.

Until suddenly, he purred, "One night. No more."

A thrill shot through her as he cast her that roguish grin.

"Who am I to say no when you beg so sweetly?"

Abruptly, his grip on her changed then, shifting from tender to bold. If she'd thought he'd been in control before, she'd been poorly mistaken.

With newfound permission, Corbin's hand dipped between her legs, cupping her pussy as if she belonged to him. "Fuck, Dani. You're wet for me," he hissed, fangs flashing as he spoke. His fingers probed her entrance with an almost fevered, wild need, but she didn't need any antici- pation, she was already so close.

Dani sunk herself down onto his hand, tearing a plea- sured groan from the vampire's lips.

"Always," she whispered. "For you, always."

Corbin's thumb found the bead of her clit with expert precision, circling it in an almost punishing way made her moan. "You put yourself in Zane's path on purpose, didn't you? Knowing I'd find you?"

Dani was panting now, her skin feeling as if she were on fire with need. "I—"

Corbin let out a guttural curse as he pushed deeper, curling his fingers up and in until they hit that delicious spot that cut her words short. Dani let out a pleasured, choked moan.

"Don't lie to me, Dani," Corbin hissed. "It doesn't suit you."

She whimpered her pleasure more as he pushed deeper into her.

But somehow, she'd known. She'd always known the heat between them would be combustible. Incomparable.

"Answer me, Dani," Corbin demanded, his free hand gripping her chin roughly.

"Yes," she panted. "Yes, I knew what I was doing."

The devious smirk that crossed Corbin's face then filled her with more pride than she'd ever known. "Clever, wicked girl," he teased.

Without warning, he pulled out of her, quickly rotating her once more until her face was pressed against the wall, the length of his cock beneath his suit pants rubbing against her bottom. Dani tried to keep her gaze low, not to look out at all the eyes hidden beneath the blurred lights of the club's glow, eyes that no doubt watched her and the vampire that pleasured her, relishing the show, but Corbin gripped a hold of her chin, forcing her to turn toward them.

"Let them see. Let them know you're mine. If only for tonight."

Dani wasn't certain what it was about those words that destroyed her so thoroughly. Whether it was how she felt as if she'd reclaimed her power, or the fact that this time, it was finally Corbin who was staking his claim of her, she didn't know. All she knew was she was about to come harder than she ever had before.

"Corbin," she panted.

"Don't be shy now, darling. Not while they're watching."

At the reminder of their audience, Dani threw back her head with a loud moan, grinding down and onto Corbin's hand. Loud enough to draw more eyes and attention toward them, but somehow, she didn't care. She was too busy riding wave after wave of pleasure on his fingers. Her pussy was absolutely soaked, beating in time with her pulse.

And he had to know.

Had to hear and feel it.

One final shudder tore through her, making her moan.

"Good girl," Corbin whispered, rubbing his hand over her clit in a way that caused her to shiver.

The last tremors of her orgasm shook through her.

He removed his hand from inside her, turning her to face him once more, before he brought his fingers to his mouth, licking each one as if to savor her taste.

"Fuck," he groaned. "You taste like the sun."

The red of his eyes was a deep garnet then, pure animal, like a predator yet...far more dangerous than anything nature could have imagined, in all the ways he drew her in, made her want to please him, though she was prey to him and little more, yet when he spoke, it was the voice of a cultured gentleman who whispered to her.

"The next time I claim you, it will be for my eyes alone. Do you understand?"

Dani nodded, still dazed from the high of her orgasm.

"One night. Nothing more," he repeated. "Are we in agreement?"

She nodded. "Nothing more," she breathed against his lips. For once, being honest about the path she chose. "But, please Corbin, I need—"

"Shhh." Corbin hushed her, placing a finger against her lips, before he whispered against her skin. "Don't tempt me more, darling." His hand cupped her chin in his palm again, his thumb tracing where he'd smeared her lipstick as he smirked once more. "Now, we've business to attend to."

4

Before Dani knew what was happening, Corbin had lifted her off the floor again, whisking her out of the club, as if she weighed no more than a feather. A blur of lights and color flashed before her eyes, until suddenly they were standing in a back alley outside the club, Corbin no longer holding her close. A luxury town car lied in wait for them.

Corbin didn't need to lift a hand to signal to the driver to pull forward, before the vehicle was already beside them, another vampire opening her door. Without hesitation, he took Dani's hand in his, ushering her into the vehicle and then rounding to the other side's door.

The town car pulled out onto Chicago's dimly lit streets moments later.

"Where are we—?"

"You choose *now* to ask questions?" Corbin cut her a perturbed look. Whatever warmth had passed between them in the club was gone now, lost in the interest of business. "Was this not your intention from the start or would you rather I leave you with, Zane?"

Dani fell silent then, wringing her hands in her lap. She knew their intimacy had been only for show, and yet...

She couldn't bring herself to regret it.

Not when it had *felt* real.

One night. Nothing more. His words echoed in her ears.

They drove across town in silence, not stopping until they'd reached one of the city's many high-rises. As soon as the car was parked, Corbin flung himself from the vehicle with supernatural speed, as if he could no longer stand to be in such a small, enclosed space with her.

Uncertain what to do, Dani followed, exiting the cab quickly, only to speed up once she'd joined him inside the lobby. Even at a normal pace, she practically had to jog to keep up with him. A doorman summoned the elevator whilst Corbin's expression remained distant, cold. He didn't even acknowledge the doorman, or her for that matter.

A small ding signaled the lift's arrival.

The elevator ride to his penthouse felt long and tense.

With each passing floor, Dani was acutely aware of every little noise she made, of the sound of her heels. Each breath she took. Of the brush of her skin against her clothes, the way she fidgeted where she stood, the sound of her pulse in her own ears. Hell, even the nearly silent sound of her tongue wetting her lips. Humans were noisy, she supposed.

Corbin, on the other hand, was silent. Painfully so.

Preternaturally still.

Like a predator lying in wait, and yet, not once, did he turn his attention toward her.

The moment the elevator doors opened, Dani practically dove out onto the main floor, desperate to be free, only to find herself standing in a handsomely decorated vestibule. There were two armed vampires waiting outside the door, identifiable from the stillness with which they stood, like sentries standing guard over their king.

Or their mafia boss, truth be told.

Corbin didn't so much as acknowledge them, before he opened the door to the penthouse and led her in, the entrance behind them falling closed with a subtle little *snick*.

Dani's breath stopped short. She'd always known the other half lived a different existence, and it wasn't as if Cillian hadn't taken her to one of his own glittering abodes, but something about specifically seeing where Corbin rested his head each night stole her breath away. Though vampires didn't need sleep, she supposed. Or at least, Cillian hadn't.

She wasn't certain whether to consider that a blessing or curse.

The inside of the penthouse was filled with modern décor, tastefully decorated, particularly so. As if its owner wasn't explicitly attempting to showcase his vast wealth, but he simply couldn't help it. The design was subtle, understated, and yet so grand in contrast to the diner and her own dingy apartment, she could hardly stand it.

"It's beautiful," Dani breathed.

Corbin didn't acknowledge her compliment. Instead, he crossed the room to the glittering window wall that overlooked the city below. He stared down at the night lights before him, as if the whole of the city were sprawled at his feet. As distant to her now as he'd been years ago. "Now, I'm assuming you plan to tell me what you were doing in my club tonight, Dani."

Dani wasn't certain what it was that made her feel brave then, as if for once, she could manage to lie and get away with it. "I'm not sure what you mean."

Corbin's cold gaze cut toward her. "Don't play coy with me, love. It only becomes you when it's genuine."

Dani swallowed. "I was there as a patron," she dared. "Nothing more."

"Bullocks." Corbin placed his hands in his pockets and leaning against the wall, though there was nothing leisurely about the piercing look he gave her. "You'll find my kindness runs thin in the face of liars and thieves, Dani."

In other words, he wouldn't stand for her to betray him, to sell him out to the Execution Underground. She known that from the start though. She owed him better than that.

Dani fell silent then, hanging her head low. How did she keep her word, stay the course when Corbin had undoubtedly been kind to her and—

As if he could read her mind, Corbin's expression turned from distant and cold to something far more fearsome. "Did that brother of yours put you up to this?"

It'd only been a matter of time before he realized, of course.

Dani gave a small nod.

At the mere mention of Quinn, Corbin swore. "Absolute bastard." He raked a rough hand through his hair, pacing a little as he muttered, "And I suppose he told you to use whatever means necessary." Corbin's eyes shot to her slender form.

As if to indicate all the places he'd touched her.

Dani's face heated. "If you're asking if that's why I let you touch me, then the answer is no." The fact that he thought that little of her hurt, frankly. Though she supposed she hadn't exactly built a reputation among the syndicate that she was proud of. "I made that choice of my own volition. I was caught up in the moment," she lied. "Take that as you will."

If Corbin cared about what had happened between them in the alcove, he didn't dare show it then. "And I suppose your brother tasked you with gathering information for him? About my holdings, my dealings, where I keep my—"

"No," she cut him off, before he revealed anything she couldn't unhear. "No, it's Lucien who's his target. Not you. Quinn just...thought you might know something, something that could point him in the right direction, that's all."

"And you believed him?" Corbin's frustration seemed to settle then. "You agreed?"

Dani shrugged. "I didn't have much of a choice."

Corbin lifted one smooth brow, prompting her to go on, but confessing how truly vulnerable she was pointed to the crux of her problem, the part she hadn't been able to fully admit to herself. "If...If Lucien decides to come for me...to... to target my brother, or worse, to retaliate against me for Cillian's death, then—"

"Then you'll need protection," he finished for her.

"Yes." She nodded.

"And your brother and his band of human thugs couldn't possibly offer that themselves?"

It wasn't her place, nor in her nature, to make excuses for the life her brother had chosen. He'd made his choice, and she'd made hers, and yet...

"Quinn says politics in the Execution Underground are...complicated right now." She shrugged her shoulders. "Apparently, there's been a split in the organization. A rift."

As if that were an excuse to throw her to the wolves. Her brother likely hadn't intended for her to share that tidbit of information, but he hadn't exactly given her much choice.

"Of course." Corbin strode closer, coming to stand in front of her, eyes no longer cold. Slowly, he reached out, tucking a stray strand of hair behind her ear. "And so, you ran to me."

Dani's breath quickened. The way he was looking at her then terrified her. It was almost...startingly in its reverence, so unlike every other version of him she'd ever seen before, and yet, still so wicked she couldn't help but consider all the things she'd beg him to do to her, if given the chance.

One night. Nothing more.

She pulled away from him then, remembering herself. "In a manner of speaking." She lowered her gaze a little, but not fast enough to miss Corbin's bemused grin.

"Clever, clever girl," he repeated.

Her eyes shot to his, searching for the pride that had settled there once before, but then his hand returned to his suit coat, leaving her standing there, alone.

As he had so many times before.

What exactly about tonight had been different?

"And what's the Execution Underground want with Lucien this time? A petty theft charge? Fraud?" Corbin sneered, making it very clear exactly what he thought of the human organization's prior efforts.

They'd failed to pin Lucien down more than once before.

"Quinn says Lucien's been trafficking human women for blood sport," Dani said, watching the club owner make his way back toward the window. "Tell me you didn't know."

Corbin didn't offer her any such comfort. He simply paused for a prolonged moment. "Must you think so little of me?"

Dani frowned. "That's not an answer, Corbin."

He turned to her, red eyes aglow. "It's being addressed."

"Being addressed?" Dani's felt herself stiffen. Everyone who'd ever had even cursory dealings with the *Cosa della notte* knew what that meant. "In other words, you're planning to make a move toward him?" To end Lucien, once and for all.

"My plans are none of your concern, *human*." Corbin's expression was so hardened then, that for once, Dani was glad for the distance between them. "But should your brother wish to end Lucien, he best get in line."

Relief coursed through her. She'd hoped Corbin wouldn't be involved, and yet, she hadn't known for certain. The vampire before her had undoubtedly done more than a few terrible things in the span of his long life, but recklessly hurting women wasn't one of them.

Corbin was above that.

Vampire or not, he didn't need to prey on the weak to keep himself from being small.

"Do you know where they are then? The locations where he's holding them?" she asked.

Corbin bristled. "That's a bold ask, Dani, even for you."

Dani fought not to roll her eyes. She doubted anyone had ever called her bold before, though she *had* just encouraged him to finger her in full view of his club, hadn't she?

Perhaps she was bolder than she gave herself credit for.

"It's what Quinn sent me for," she added. "The locations of the drop houses."

"A lofty task, if not unmanageable."

Dani stepped forward, ever hopeful. "Does that mean you'll help me then?"

"After that little show at the club, I'm not certain I have a choice, do I?"

Something inside her prickled at his words, but whatever emotion she was feeling, she pushed it down. To that place that held any hint of defiance or self-defense. Like she had so many times before. Such hope for the future had gotten her nowhere. Had never helped her. "So, you meant it then? That I'm yours? That I'm under your protection?" she whispered.

"Make no mistake, Dani. I meant every word." The red glow of Corbin's eyes cut toward her as he unbuttoned his suit coat, stripping down to his only shirt. He rolled the sleeves up to his elbows, exposing the muscled forearm below. "Until this is over, you're mine and mine alone. Do I make myself clear?" he asked, looking directly toward her.

And I will do everything within my power to keep you safe.

He didn't say the words and yet, she heard them all the same, as if she'd wished them into existence. All she had to do was agree.

She repeated the phrase in her mind, mulling the words over.

Until this is over.

Which meant...

Which meant this really wasn't permanent. It was still for show. A fake. Exactly as he'd told her before, and as for what happened between them...

It truly had been a one-time occurrence. Nothing more.

She couldn't help but feel a bit...put out by that.

"And what do you get out of this? What do you gain by helping me?"

"The pleasure of your company for an evening, nothing more," he answered.

She wanted to believe him, but she couldn't help but feel as if there were something he wasn't saying.

"Do we have an agreement?" Corbin prompted.

"Yes," she said, unable to say anything more.

Corbin had helped her, protected her, so why couldn't she shake the feeling that she'd just made a deal with devil?

"Good. Come." Corbin beckoned her forward, drawing her thoughts to a close.

Dani accepted the reprieve, following him further into the penthouse and through a short series of halls and doors, until finally, he stopped at the farthest end of the row. A room tucked away like secret. Corbin turned the handle, holding open the door like any human gentleman, though they both knew he was something more.

More dangerous, more beautiful. Just more.

Dani stepped inside, taking in the sight of the immaculate bedroom. The soft down of the bed, the marbled floors, and a fireplace that in the winter she would have loved to read by to keep warm, all working together to paint a portrait of comfort and luxury.

"You'll sleep here." Corbin turned to leave then, moving to close the door.

"What about Lucien?" she said, placing her hand against it.

Corbin lifted a brow at where her hand stayed his movement.

Instantly, she dropped it to her side again, eyes falling low, as an embarrassed blush filled her cheeks. "What I mean is...without information to give to Quinn, I...I won't be safe," she clarified. "Not in the long-term."

Corbin's gaze fell to the blush on her cheeks, and had she not kept her eyes low, she might have missed the subtle writhe of the muscles at his throat, despite that his expression remained unmoving, disinterested.

Perhaps he *did* want her. Or a taste of her at least.

So, what game was he playing at?

"Lucien's hosting a party at his home tomorrow. Play your role, and you'll have your revenge. Leave the details to me." Corbin turned to leave then, but she stopped him once more.

This time, with a gentle hand on his arm.

"Corbin, I...I'm not certain I can face him again. The last time I saw Lucien, he—"

Corbin's dark gaze pierced through her. "The shame is his. Not yours." He captured her chin, forcing her to look at him. "Don't forget that." He let her go.

Dani swallowed, trying and failing to rid the tears that gathered at the edge of her eyes.

"And your plan?" she asked.

"We'll discuss the plan later, once you've rested." He turned to leave again.

"Thank you, Corbin. Really," she whispered. She really was grateful to him, even if she didn't yet know what to make her decision to trust him.

"Don't thank me. Not until this is over." He moved to leave once more, but this time, it was his turn to hesitate. "And Dani."

"Mmmm?" she hummed from where she'd flitted over to the bed. She was suddenly so tired she could hardly stand it, sleep calling to her.

Corbin cast her a cursory glance over his shoulder. "Next time that coward you call a brother sends you in his place again, I'll kill him where he stands."

Dani nodded. "Noted."

She slipped into bed just as Corbin closed the door, quickly settling into the sheets.

For once, Dani fell asleep the moment her head hit the pillow, falling into a deep and peaceful slumber that was better than she'd had in far too many years before, restful in the assurance that, at least for tonight, no one would hurt her.

Not if Corbin had anything to say about it.

"WE'VE BEEN through this before, Zane." Corbin glared at the vampire pinned against his desk inside The Blood Rose. The bastard's nose already bleeding, Zane's face battered and bruised from where Corbin's men had delivered the other vampire to his office hours ago. Once Dani was asleep, Corbin had only returned to ensure this situation was handled, personally.

"I *said*, how many times must I ask you to keep your hands to yourself, Zane?" Corbin roared, slamming his fist down onto the desk beside Zane's head.

The other vampire flinched. "I told you I won't touch her again, Corbin. Fuck! I swear it," Zane pleaded. Zane was smashed flat and straining against the wood of Corbin's desk, where Fox and Luciano held him down, hands restrained behind his back. Blood trickled from his nose, staining the starch white legal pad beneath his cheek.

"I...I didn't know she was yours. It won't happen again."

"Mine or not, your task was simple." Corbin crouched low, coming eye-to-eye with the other vampire. Even though they were brethren, they were united by species alone. Zane wasn't a part of the family. Of Corbin's branch of the *Cosa della notte*. He wasn't even among one of the other four with whom they were constantly at war. No, Zane was no better than the filth beneath Corbin's shoes and unwilling to keep his hands to himself to boot.

That much was clear.

"Leave the humans in my club alone. Do you understand?" Corbin hissed.

"Yes! Yes, I understand," Zane panted, this face quickly

turning red, from anger and shame rather than lack of oxygen. Vampires didn't *need* to breathe.

A fact that made torture far more complicated.

"Good." Corbin stood again, nodding to Fox and Luciano.

Luciano released one of Zane's hands, bringing his flattened palm forth along with the stake and the hammer that would soon go with it.

Corbin plucked the stake off the table, aligning it over Zane's palm. "Now the next time you get handsy with one of my patrons again, you'll remember it."

Zane thrashed, suddenly realizing exactly where this was going as Fox stepped forward, menacing the hammer in one meaty fist.

"No. No! Please, Corbin! I—"

Corbin ignored the other vampire's pleas, driving the first blow in. Zane roared, his blood spattering across Corbin's desk as the stake drove through tender tendons. Corbin took his fill, his pleasure at the sight of Zane's pain, before casting the hammer onto the floor.

Fox handed him a towel for his hands.

"Clean it up once you've finished," he ordered, abandoning the task to his men.

Wiping his palms clean, he cast the towel aside, before he closed his office door, smoothing a rough hand down his shirt as he sealed off the sound of Zane's continued screams from the few remaining patrons below. It was nearly past close, though the music thumping from the floors below still provided adequate coverage.

"That was a bit excessive," Kharis murmured to his right, "even for you." The ancient Greek leaned against the hallway wall, a lit cigarette in his hand as he waited for him.

"Your point?" Corbin lowered his shirt sleeves, buttoning

his cufflinks. Thankfully, he hadn't gotten any blood on his shirt this time. Bloodstains were a beast to clean.

"My point is that one good finger fuck, and she's already gotten under your skin."

Corbin scowled, flashing fang. "I thought we discussed this earlier, Kharis. Underboss or no, stay *out* of my sex life."

"I'll make it a point when you stop fingering helpless humans in full view of your club for show." Kharis gave him a pointed look, before taking a long pull.

Corbin smirked. "Enjoyed that now, did you?" he taunted.

"You're shameless. Truly." Kharis flicked the ashes of his cigarette, stubbing out the ember it left on the carpet with his toe. "We're this close." Kharis made a pinching gesture with his fingers. "This close and you're going to let your feelings for some human cunt get in the way."

The lust for violence that filled Corbin then had little to do with being a vampire. Its grip on his psyche sharp and fierce. "Speak of her like that again, and friend or no, you'll find yourself in a similar position to Zane," he warned. Corbin's eyes flashed crimson, making the seriousness of his threat clear. "No one understands how close we are better than I do. You think I don't know?"

Kharis fell silent for a beat, the glow of his cigarette pulsating in the dark.

"She's distraction. Nothing more," Corbin reassured.

"For you or Lucien?" Kharis sneered.

"Both." Corbin's eyes narrowed. "I don't see a point in the distinction."

Kharis cast the butt of his cigarette onto the carpet. "And what's your plan tomorrow when your sire attempts to hold her close? Whispers in her ear? What will you do then?" The Greek lifted a brow. "What you did to Zane?"

"Call him by that title again and true death will be yours before morning," Corbin hissed, crimson gaze aflame. "Lucien doesn't need to touch her. He only needs to look, to be tempted."

"If you think he won't want a taste of her in a show of good faith, you're a fool." Kharis waved a dismissive hand.

"And what *exactly* do you suggest as an alternative?" Corbin lifted a brow. "Use her as bait?"

Kharis crossed his arms over his chest, leaning against the wall again with a shrug. "In not so blunt of terms."

For a moment, Corbin dared consider it, before finally, he shook his head. "No. No, we stick to the plan."

"Which is?"

"She serves as a distraction, and Lucien need not touch her."

"And when this is over?" Kharis prompted.

"I let her go."

His friend chuckled. "If you say so."

"I *do* say so," Corbin said, eyes narrowing again.

"And the information she requested? In exchange?"

Corbin shook his head. "She's not going to get it. Not before Lucien is dead, that is." He moved to brush past Kharis, to return to his apartment before the sun rose. He needed to escape the overpowering scent of sex, of blood and tobacco that lingered inside the club. He had no intention of being cooped up here. Not all day. "That's all she truly wants anyway."

"For your sake, Corbin, I hope you're right."

Corbin simply nodded in response, before he disappeared into the club's ether, blending amongst the shadows. He was a true creature of the night. A swath of darkness without a soul.

He didn't pause until he was out in the streets below,

climbing into the back of the town car again. His eyes settled on the orange rim of the sunrise just beyond on the Chicago skyline.

For the last hundred years, he'd worked toward this moment, to when he could finally take his revenge, and as Kharis had reminded him, it was supposed to taste sweet. As sweet as the sun had once felt upon his face as he'd watched it rise each morn. Never once had he questioned whether it was worth the sacrifice.

But for once, Corbin felt himself hesitate.

5

Dani didn't wake until the following evening, the events and uncertainty of the previous night having worn through her. Even working the midnight shift at the diner as she often did, she'd severely underestimated exactly how much vampiric hours took their toll.

Finally awake, she sat up in bed, quickly casting the covers off as her eyes searched through the dark. The dimly lit glow of the club's neon lights from the night prior lingered behind her eyes, the constant thump of its music still ringing in her ears. Coupled with the hypervigilance she was forced to exert every time she was in a vampire's presence—a heightened level of awareness to which she no longer accustomed to—the combination proved more than a little tiresome.

But Dani was nothing if not a survivor.

She stood from the bed, flicking on the bedside light as she went.

Only to let out a startled shriek.

Corbin sat in an armchair on the far side of the room,

one long leg propped across the other where he sat frozen in wait of her, like a king who'd been waiting for a rather long time for his consort to wake. Though what was a few passing hours to an immortal?

"Get dressed," he said, before quickly exiting the room, leaving nothing but those two words and a dark blur of movement within his wake.

Dani's gaze fell to the edge of the bed. To the black dress bag which waited.

Play your role and in exchange, you'll have your revenge, he'd said.

Wasn't that always the path she chose to take?

The path of least resistance.

Though she was straddling uncharted territory here.

Unzipping the dress bag, Dani took her time getting ready, pleased, and yet not surprised, to find the clutch she'd abandoned at the club the night before had been retrieved for her. It waited on the bathroom's granite counter, filled with all the makeup she could possibly need. Not to mention, a fresh toothbrush. She never left home unprepared.

When she finally emerged, dressed and ready, Corbin was waiting for her by the walled window, overlooking the glittering city below. "Hello, darling," he purred, the smooth timber of his voice sending a little thrum of excitement through her. "You look lovely."

His gaze raked over her.

The dress he'd left for her fit like a dream. A gold silk ballgown, finer than anything she'd ever worn, with a stunning draped neckline and a scandalously low, plunging back that brought out the sun kissed undertones of her skin and hair.

It made her feel like she was a golden goddess, her beauty beaming.

For a moment, Dani allowed herself to bask in his attention, to pretend this wasn't all a dream. "Thank you," she whispered. Some small part of her was convinced that if she spoke too loudly, she might break the spell between them.

"Shall we take our leave?" Corbin said, offering her his arm.

Oh, so gentlemanly.

Except when he wasn't.

Like when they'd been in alone in the alcove.

She ducked her head, hiding a knowing grin.

Corbin was dressed in a three-piece suit that had clearly been tailored for him it fit him so well, like a glove, highlighting all the parts of him she'd once wished to explore.

Parts she *still* wished to explore, if she was being honest.

With her hands, her tongue, her teeth.

One night. Nothing more.

Coarse words and yet, they served their purpose.

To remind her of how little she truly meant to him. Even if he'd offered her this favor, this chance at revenge.

Dani accepted his arm, following him out of the penthouse and down to the street below, where the town car already waited.

It wasn't until they were sealed securely inside, the partition window up and the silence growing tense between them that Corbin finally spoke.

"Lucien keeps the current locations of the drop houses written in a journal inside his office. You'll find it located to the right of the third-floor stairs."

Dani lifted a brow. "How do you—?"

"Where I get my information isn't your concern." Corbin shot her a look. "When I give you the signal, make your way upstairs, unnoticed. You'll find it unlocked. Don't hesitate when I give you the signal. Just go."

Dani inhaled a long breath, steeling herself. "It's that simple?"

Corbin tsked his tongue at her, as if she were being a fool. "It's both that simple and that difficult, Dani." He faced toward her then, his eyes growing dark. A reminder of the violence he chose to surround himself with. "Because if you get caught, may God have mercy on you, since Lucien certainly won't."

They continued the rest of the ride in silence, the blurred neon lights and concrete scenery of the city soon fading into the trimmed shrubs and manicured lawns of the suburbs. The car didn't stop until they'd reached a secluded mansion, a line of limousines and other town cars queued around the circular drive for the black-tie event.

"Play your role, Dani," Corbin said. "That's all you have to do."

Dani's heart was suddenly pounding in her ears, her palms sweaty.

Corbin reached for the door.

But before she realized what she was doing, Dani lunged for him, staying his hand.

Corbin's eyes narrowed, his lip curling a little as if he were preparing to tell her she'd overstepped.

"Corbin, I...I'm not certain I can do this."

The whole thing had seemed so manageable from the safety of Corbin's penthouse, or when he'd held her in his arms, but now that they were here, the thought of facing Lucien again, even though she'd requested Corbin's help with this, it...

Corbin must have recognized what she was thinking,

because something inside him seemed to melt then, his gaze softening.

It was almost too much to bear.

"What can I do to convince you of your power?" he whispered.

"My power?" Dani's eyes widened as she blinked.

Corbin smirked a little as if she'd amused him. "Come now, Dani, you're not naïve. You must see the way men look at you, women too."

Dani glanced down at her hands. "As if I am a prize to be claimed, or a...a threat to be eliminated."

"Exactly," Corbin flashed her a devilish grin. "There is power in captivating attention, in being the most beautiful woman in the room, in deciding when and to whom you gift your attention. You need not have a blade to cut a man down with a single look."

Dani's breath felt heavy now, her chest rising and falling with the quickening of her pulse as she hung on his every word. Is that how he saw her?

As someone who could be powerful?

Who could be fierce enough to wield beauty as a weapon?

"Now, what can I do to help you claim that power for yourself?"

She was nearly drunk from the high of his words, his unfaltering belief in her. She could feel it beneath her skin. Like being glamoured, and yet, so much better. So much more.

It was intoxicating.

But could she trust it?

Dani met his eyes. She desperately wanted to.

"Just...Just don't leave my side, please." She gripped his

arm, fortifying herself a little. "Not until I have to go upstairs, that is."

Corbin smiled then, more relaxed and genuine than she'd seen in years. "Dani, only a fool would dare leave your side willingly. Tonight, you are mine, and I intend to ensure everyone knows it."

Dani's eyes widened. "With more public sex?" she nearly squeaked.

Corbin chuckled, smirking a little, before he gripped her hand, brushing a gentle kiss across it as they exited the vehicle. "Don't tempt me, darling," he whispered, "because tonight you're mine, and the evening is young yet."

Thus far, the party was far more manageable than Dani had anticipated, the hours passing by quickly in a blur of posh outfits, shimmering chandeliers, delicious hors d'oeuvres and glittering dances. For once, it was easy being there among the crowd, latched onto Corbin's arm as he charmed his way through conversation after conversation.

He was undeniably good at this, at communicating, conversing, charming anyone and everyone in his wake, exactly as he'd urged her to do. So good that watching him for so long felt a little like she'd been staring into the sun for the whole of the evening. Given long enough, she could almost be singed by the sheer magnitude of it. Watching him made her forget herself.

What wonders could he accomplish if he chose to use those skills for the greater good?

The possibilities were endless, really.

By the time Dani was finally able to catch her breath, the

evening was already halfway through, though they'd still yet to encounter Lucien. Not that she was looking forward to it.

Dani knew when the time came.

Corbin's gaze flicked toward her, his dark eyes finding hers, where they stood together among the hallway's glittering vestibules. "Brace yourself," he whispered, giving her a moment to prepare.

As much as she could ever be prepared anyway.

There was no way for Dani to accurately describe how she felt in that moment, seeing the face of a man, a vampire who'd decided to rape her, who in a single act had chosen to wreak untold havoc and devastation in her life. Nausea, anxiety, panic, she'd experienced all that and more leading up to the months, the moments that led her here. The mere notion of being in the same room as him made her feel physically ill. Terrified. Sick.

Her stomach flipped, revolting against her, and for a moment, it felt as if she'd been lifted out of her body, no more than a viewer at the stunned woman who stood below, a beautiful woman, an ethereal beauty she soon recognized as herself, but then, almost as quickly as the feeling overtook her, it was gone, replaced instead by a sudden warmth as Corbin whispered to her.

"Breathe, darling."

Dani sucked in a harsh pull of air.

Without hesitation, Corbin swept her out of sight, to the far side of the room, hiding them both away where no one could see them. This time, nothing about his touch was meant for show. It wasn't even sexual ...

This was for and her alone.

For her reassurance. Her fortitude.

"Listen to me," Corbin hissed, instantly commanding her attention. "There is no right or wrong way to respond to choosing to face someone who's assaulted you, Dani," he said, his voice caught between a heated whisper and a thinly veiled snarl at the thought of what'd happened to her, "and nothing I say can take away the pain, the panic or rage you may feel at seeing him in public like this.

"But you and you alone are in control of what happens next. *You* get to choose how to respond, whether you will face him, brazen and confident as I know you can be, as you claim your revenge, or whether you will choose to cower in fear. That choice will never be his to make. Do I make myself clear?"

Dani nodded slightly, unable to bring herself to speak or look at him.

Corbin cupped her cheek gently. "I've asked too much of you, suggesting you come here. I see that clearly now. I apologize for not seeing it sooner. We need only—"

"No," Dani said, inhaling a sharp breath, forcing herself to breathe through her fear. "No, I asked this of you. I...I need to do this." She shook her head a little. "I *want* to do this," she corrected herself. "To face him, to show him that he couldn't break me."

She glanced up at Corbin then.

It would have been easy to blame how she'd gotten here on her brother, or even on Corbin, for all the ways their personalities often and easily overtook hers. But neither had forced her hand or taken away her decision. Not as Cillian and Lucien did.

Tonight, the choice had been hers and hers alone.

She'd been the one who intended this.

And there was an...oddly satisfying power in that. In reclaiming this unusual, glittering life from which she'd been driven away. For better or worse.

Enough that for once, she felt she could be brave, despite her fear.

"I'm ready now," she said, lifting her gaze to Corbin's again. "I want to face him."

The look Corbin gave her was one filled with respect. "You have more courage than anyone gives you credit for, Dani, and I think," Corbin shook his head a little, like it killed him to admit it, "I think that blasted brother of yours may have seen that from the start." Corbin extended his arm toward her. "Shall we?"

Dani took hold of him, gently bringing him close. "After you."

Corbin led her forward, steering her in the direction of an adjacent crowd, as if he hoped to buy her more time, give her a reprieve to gather herself for a moment more, but Dani took a harsher hold on him, surprised when the vampire allowed her to lead them both.

"I need to get this over with," she whispered.

The second time she laid eyes on Lucien wasn't as jarring at the first, but if she'd thought she had conquered her queasiness, the sight of the human woman leashed like a dog at his feet immediately corrected her misassumption. She'd once been treated the same with Cillian.

Her stomach plummeted.

"I think I might be sick," she whispered to Corbin, just before Lucien stepped forward.

"Then I'd recommend you aim for his godawful excuse of a suit," Corbin muttered, forcing her to let out an unlady-like snort.

"Corbin, so good of you to come," Lucien purred.

"I wouldn't have missed it for the world," Corbin said, his manners perfectly intact, but there was an...underlying maliciousness in his tone that Dani wasn't certain anyone else could hear. Not unless they dared to look for it.

Corbin's disdain for Lucien was clear.

So clear that, if Dani didn't know better, she would have said Corbin's dislike of Lucien was personal. More than a hate between two feuding mafia bosses. More than the protective instinct he might feel for Lucien's victims, or for her as a friend, if that's even what they could be considered. No, the lust for violence in Corbin's eyes wasn't even slightly circumstantial.

It was intimate, ancient, fierce.

Fueled by a hatred birthed long, long ago.

Longer than she'd ever have a chance to live.

The difference between them struck her starkly then, making her suddenly aware of who and what he was. She wasn't certain how she hadn't seen it before.

Even *if* Corbin had offered her more than one night, made her sweet promises, Corbin Blackwell was as beautiful of a being as he was old, a creature meant to outlast her. He was ancient, unchanging, and as twisted as he was fierce, frozen in time like a film reel. Moving, and yet, not fully alive either.

Not breathing. Not flesh as she was.

Not human.

And yet, she wanted that kind of power, the power that came with an unending existence.

Is *that* what had always brought her here? To this glittering world? A search for power? For immortality? Along with the revenge she now wished.

And if so, what kind of monster did that make her?

Dani swallowed hard, her tongue instantly dry and thick. Maybe Quinn was right. Maybe she *had* turned her back on humanity.

She reached for the long chain of her necklace, cradled between her breasts. She pulled it from her decolletage, fingering the skeleton key there for strength. At the sight of it, Corbin's eyes went wide, his nostrils flaring, but Dani didn't have time to question it, before the fleeting look was gone in an instant.

She blinked, vaguely aware that Lucien was now talking to her. "I'm sorry. Were you saying something?" she said, turning down her nose at him.

She couldn't help but notice Corbin's smirk at the corner of her eye as Lucien sneered.

"Perhaps you'd prefer to put your pet on a leash," Lucien said to Corbin whilst staring straight through her. "Then she might be better trained."

Corbin's look of feigned boredom was an immediate dismissal. "I don't need to keep my companions on a leash in order to tame them, Lucien. Personally, I find they are more than eager to return of their own free will." Corbin placed a hand on her lower back, drawing her to him, protecting her once more.

"Why bother to amuse them when you can simply take?" Lucien said, his disgusting gaze raking over her.

Adrenaline shot through Dani, making her unable to stop herself. "A man only steals what he cannot win fairly." She turned her attention toward Corbin then, forcing more than a little admiration into her gaze. Gently, she reached out, cradling his cheek. "Stealing is beneath you. It's the tactic of the poor and desperate." She turned her gaze toward Lucien then. She stepped back a little. "Lovely party. Now, if you'll excuse me."

Dani made a hasty exit then, escaping the pressing heat of the ballroom and quickly locating a passing waiter. She plucked a bubbling champagne glass from his tray, before immediately downing the contents. She felt Corbin's presence behind her a moment later.

"I think you're supposed to savor it," he whispered into her ear.

Dani passed the champagne flute back to the waiter, before snatching another. "I'm sorry I insulted him so blatantly. I have no doubt that'll cause trouble for you, but I…I just couldn't stand to stay silent as he stood there with that smug look on his face, and that poor woman…"

"Do you think I am angry with you?" Corbin asked, as if he were amused.

Dani shook her head a little, sipping more of her champagne glass. Now that she was really letting the flavor linger in her mouth, she wasn't even certain she truly wanted it. She set the half-full flute down on another passing tray again. "I just thought maybe you'd be—"

"You were incredible, darling, and Lucien is no doubt furious. You have his attention now, and that's exactly where we want him."

Dani lifted a brow. "And *why* do we want his attention again?"

Corbin had never exactly made that clear.

He hadn't been very forthcoming about their plans. A fact that hadn't escaped her attention.

He chuckled a little, as if she'd done something to amuse him again. "Like I said before," he extended his arm toward her. "You'll have your revenge. Leave the details to me."

Dani hummed her approval. The champagne going to her head quickly, relaxing her. Just enough to make her forget, if for a moment, that she couldn't fully trust him.

Not really.

He was still a vampire after all. As her brother had reminded her.

The growing tension and feeling between them nothing more than for show.

Hiccupping, she held Corbin tight as he led her back toward the dance floor. "Now that you've proven to this world that you're unafraid of Lucien, time to reclaim your place as its queen," he said, his words enticing and entrancing her once more.

To her surprise, for the next hour, Dani didn't once think of Lucien again, or, if she was truthful, she managed to avoid looking at him directly, at least. Instead, she was too caught up in the feel of what it was like to be whisked about the dance floor in Corbin's arms, to have all eyes watching her. Even if it wasn't real. Even though it never would be.

And though she knew that in time, Corbin would give her the signal to slip away, to take her true shot against Lucien, already she felt as if she had won, because tonight, she'd learned what she'd came here to do. To reassert herself. To reclaim her place.

And survival was its own kind of revenge entirely.

6

T he hour grew late, and for once in his very long life, Corbin was starting to become nervous. "Where are they?" he hissed, pulling Kharis to the side whilst Dani had ducked into the ladies' room.

"There here now. Just arrived," Kharis confirmed.

A weight lifted from Corbin's chest. "Good." He nodded. "Good."

They needed more than a little finesse, if this was to go smoothly.

"And Lucien?" Kharis asked, quirking a brow. The Greek's dark eyes combed the room, as if in search for the vampire in question.

"Intrigued," Corbin said, his gaze narrowing to where Dani now crossed the room toward them. "And none the wiser. He hasn't been able to take his eyes off her all evening."

"Good," Kharis said. He made a show of clapping Corbin on the shoulder. "We may just pull this off, old boy."

"Don't get too confident," Corbin warned, as Dani approached. "Not yet."

"Too confident about what?" she asked, those large doe-eyes staring up at him.

Fuck, she made him wish he were an honest man. A *good* man.

It really did kill him that he had to use her this way, to treat her as if she and her goals didn't mean anything to him, but it was par for the course, he supposed. He was a vampire, and she was a human, and everything good in his life had already been taken from him.

Dani was simply one thing more.

Another of his men walked past them then, nodding to Kharis, who returned the gesture. Kharis faced Corbin, lowering his voice to a whisper. "They're in position now."

Dani's brow furrowed. "Who's in position?"

If Corbin didn't know better, he would have said she was growing suspicious of him. Well, within the past moments, at least.

"Nothing, darling," Corbin said, lying through his teeth, as he pulled her to him, into another intimate embrace. The way she melted against him either showed her adoration for him was genuine, or else, Dani was a far better actress than he gave her credit for.

Over top her head, he shot Kharis a harsh look, before he laid a kiss within the soft span between her throat and her cheek. She smelled of the sun, and summer rain, of honeysuckle and every daytime delight he'd once held dear. The woman was temptation incarnate.

Goddamn, he was a right bastard, betraying her trust like this.

But he'd worked too long, too hard not to see this through.

His own revenge took precedence.

"Now's your cue, darling," he whispered. "Godspeed."

To Dani's credit, she played her role well, meeting his kiss with a tender peck of her own, her soft, red lips brushing against the barely there stubble of his jaw. Her hand trailed over the curve of his bicep, down the arm of his suit coat, and to his fingers, where she lingered there, holding onto him briefly, as if she were inviting him to a private rendezvous. As if she couldn't bring herself to part with him, for even a moment.

Corbin grumbled his approval, his fangs aching at the sight, his cock growing hard.

Fuck, she was making this difficult.

Everything with Dani had always been difficult.

She slipped into the ballroom's ether, as at home among the beauty and the harsh cruelty which lay beneath the facade as any one of them. She was a part of this world, and yet, not.

Not in the ways that truly mattered.

"Are you certain you want to do this?" Kharis asked from beside him.

Corbin nodded. "We've been through this. We stick to the plan."

Kharis lifted a brow. "And if the plan means you no longer get to enjoy your little human? If she hates you for it?"

Corbin swallowed, hard. Some sacrifices were worth making, and already he'd sacrificed more than a century. What was one thing more?

"Tell Orpheus to stick to the plan," he said, "And if Dani gets in the way, then so be it."

Better she be dead than continue to make him feel.

To remember everything he'd tried so hard to forget.

∿

RIDING a high from the thrills of the evening, Dani snaked her way across the dance floor, making her way toward the stairs without fear. All she had to do was slip quietly upstairs, undetected, and then she was home free. She was in the home stretch, almost there now, so close she could taste it, when suddenly, a sharp hand tugged at her wrist.

She rolled her eyes. This was getting old quickly.

She turned, expecting to find Zane again like she had in the club the night before, but instead, it was Lucien who held her in his grip.

Instantly, Dani's blood ran cold.

"He doesn't know I've already had you before, does he?" Lucien hissed, the hate in his words sharp enough to pierce. "He doesn't know that I've already had my way with you?"

Dani twisted toward him, spitting into his face. "Fuck you!" she shouted.

She wouldn't be manhandled anymore.

She was no longer anyone's plaything.

Every pair of eyes in the room fell toward them then, the attention of every partygoer coming to a halt. Whether it was because someone had dared spit in Lucien's face, or because it'd been *her* who'd been the offender that wasn't clear.

She was known to be docile. Meek.

A glittering prize to be won.

Not a queen like Corbin painted her to be, though she was behaving as one now.

What was happening to her?

Her eyes combed the crowd then, already knowing the answer she'd find there. She may not have been certain she could trust him, at least not completely, but Corbin's belief in her had been unfaltering, his actions tonight and the previous evening backed up by all the times he'd saved her before. Trusting him hadn't been without president.

Her eyes settled on him then, the look in his gaze stopping her breath instantly.

Fury was what she expected to find there, a protective instinct as he played the king at her side once more. She'd expected him to shield her, to protect like he always did.

Instead, the look he gave her was one of apology.

As if to say, *I didn't want to betray you.*

And yet he had, hadn't he?

But how?

Her eyes shot toward Lucien then, to where he gripped her in an unbreakable hold, and then to Corbin's men about the room, the almost choreographed way they moved, as if they were all gears of a turning clock, sliding into place at Corbin's will, causing the hour chime to sound, and *she* was his Cinderella, forced to go home. Her slippers suddenly ill fit.

The clock chimed. All the pieces falling into place.

But Dani didn't hear it.

She was too busy feeling the way in which her heart shattered, her eyes falling to the nine-millimeter at Corbin's side as, at his behest, the first rounds of gunshots shattered the windows.

As he claimed her revenge, as if it were his own.

FUCKING HELL! She was supposed to have made it to the safety of the upstairs, damn it, and now, he wasn't supposed to move.

Corbin had been instructed to stay where he was. To be the first to drop to the ground, signaling to all his men in the room to do the same, shielding themselves from the crucifix laden bullets that would no doubt leave them all bleeding upon the marble floor whilst true death lingered near. But in the mixture of careful planning and the evening's chaotic fray, he'd failed to account for his own feelings.

Feelings for the human woman, who'd already gotten too near.

The fear he felt the moment he'd looked in Dani's eyes overtook him in an instant, though he no longer saw a cowering, innocent woman there. Instead, she was furious, a breathtaking harpy out for vengeance.

Vengeance against him. For betraying her. For lying to her.

For stealing her revenge.

Her hatred for him was clear. And if Corbin didn't act now, he was certain to regret it.

Though the hit had already been cleared.

He was running toward Dani then, before he even realized he was moving, tackling her to the ground to protect her from the onslaught.

And giving Lucien the split second of warning that he needed.

At supernatural speed, Lucien spun, grabbing the human woman he'd forced to trail him and falling to his knees behind her. He used her body as if it were shield. As if she were cannon fodder. No better or worse than he'd nearly done to Dani.

Corbin felt instantly sick.

Except Dani was on the floor beneath him now, her fragile body hidden beneath his as a continuous spray of bullets rained down upon them, her mouth hanging open as if she were screaming, though the sounds of more than one semi-automatic made it impossible to hear.

But that didn't matter now. She was safe. Alive, even if she hated him.

And Corbin still wasn't ready to give up his revenge just yet.

With Dani still pinned beneath him, he slung his other arm over his head like a buffer. His gaze darted toward Lucien, where the ancient vampire now attempted to worm his way out beneath the continuous spray of bullets, army crawling amongst the blood and bodies that littered the floor. Bodies Corbin held little concern for.

"Kharis!" he bellowed, his voice barely audible above the spray of gunfire.

Gunfire that he'd ordered. That he'd planned for from the beginning. Long before Dani had become a part of it.

Kharis was already moving, striding forward with a semi-automatic, prepared to take the shot for him. The Greek shifted the metal of his magazine, slipping it into gear.

From beneath him, Dani screamed. "No!"

She saw what was coming, even before Corbin did.

The moment Kharis pulled the trigger, barely breathing, the leashed human woman leaped in front of Lucien once more, eyes glazed from where she'd been glamoured, manipulated into taking one final bullet for him.

Lucien had known. He'd fucking known.

Corbin roared his fury.

The bullet pierced straight between the woman's eyes, killing her in an instant. As Dani would have been forced to do for Cillian once before.

Dani shrieked from beneath him, bucking wildly, like an injured beast wishing to be put out of her misery. Or wishing to kill him. He wasn't certain, which of her priorities came first.

For a moment, Corbin's eyes were drawn to her, but then Kharis was shouting at him, the sound ringing in his ears.

"Corbin!"

He had a shot. Lucien's back was wide open. This was his chance.

Corbin staggered to his feet, lifting his gun and taking his aim.

This was it. Everything he'd waited a century for.

But he hadn't accounted for the woman at his side. The one who, now free, lunged at him, clawing at his face.

"How could you? How could you?" Dani shrieked, as she knocked his aim askew.

His gun fired too far to the right, decimating his aim.

Still, the bullet caught Lucien in his lower back.

But one bullet wasn't enough to keep down an ancient vampire as powerful and old as Lucien. He would manage to get away, past Corbin's other men, running like the coward he was then.

Corbin swayed where he stood, covered in blood, his hair littered in glass shards, shaking from head to toe. Dani lay on the ground at his feet then, though he wasn't quite certain how she'd gotten there. She was screaming still, guttural, heart wrenching cries where she lay on his Armani shoes. Corbin didn't glance toward her, vaguely realizing he'd never smelled the scent of human tears before.

They tasted like sorrow and melancholy, and every ounce of grief he'd ever tried to forget. Or maybe, it was simply *Dani's* tears.

One more way in which she was destroying him.

Kharis moved toward him. "Corbin, he—"

"Find him," Corbin hissed, his eyes crazed. "Find him! Did you hear me?" he roared.

Those of his men who were still standing, which was

thankfully, all but a few, moved into action, whilst Kharis and Fox began to stake any vampire still alive in the room, any among them who wasn't their own. It took more than a few bullets to end them.

Corbin swayed a little.

At his feet, Dani whimpered. "How could you? How could you?"

Coming to Corbin's side, Luciano lifted her, gripping hold of Dani to subdue her, but she thrashed against him, struggling and screaming.

"Let 'er go, Lu," Corbin ordered. "Let 'er go," he said, a hint of Birmingham slipping into his tone for the first time in several decades, though he'd worked to hide it for centuries, to sound like a British gentleman.

Not a boy from the Birmingham slums.

The moment Luciano released her, Dani charged toward him like she'd claw off his face if she got a chance. But Corbin caught her wrists in his, loosening his hold only enough to allow her to settle for a right hook. The blow she landed was quick and efficient, like her brother had no doubt taught her. His nose was even bleeding a little.

"I suppose I deserved that," he said, swiping away the blood at his nose. "I'm a bad man, Dani. I'm a bad man and you best get yourself out of 'ere."

"Corbin," Kharis said.

Corbin lifted a hand. "Not now, Kharis. Can't you see I'm—"

"Corbin," Kharis shouted once more.

But Corbin wasn't looking toward his friend. Instead, his eyes fell to Dani, to how she'd lost all the fight she had in her eyes only a moment ago.

Instead, she was staring down at her own dress, the golden silk covered in blood, her gaze wild and frantic, as she searched for wounds and found none. Mouth gaping, those wild eyes darted from her chest to his own.

Corbin glanced down then, realizing it was *his* blood dripping onto the floor, coating Dani's dress from where he'd been peppered in bullets. All in a foolish attempt to shield her.

Though the damage had already been done.

That one unplanned move had cost him everything.

He blinked, swaying a little as he looked up once more. The world spun, tilting as Fox and Kharis moved toward him, and Corbin passed out with little more than a grimly muttered,

"Fuck."

7

C orbin lay in the dark with his eyes closed as sleep failed to claim him. Unconsciousness had done so only briefly, but even that moment of respite had done little to abate his mounting frustration with himself.

What the fuck had he been thinking?

"You were healed hours ago, but you couldn't be bothered to face your own fucked decisions, could you?" Kharis' voice came from where he stood near the door.

Corbin opened his eyes then, staring up at the ceiling, a bottle of whiskey clutched in his hand, though he didn't bother to look at Kharis.

Not until he'd solved this massive clusterfuck he'd created for himself.

"I warned you," Kharis said, speaking once more. "I warned you this might happen and yet you failed to listen." Kharis pushed away from the wall near which he stood, stalking across Corbin's bedroom toward him. "Stay out of my sex life, Kharis," he mocked. "She won't be a problem, Kharis." The underboss shook his head as he roared, "Like fucking hell she will!"

Corbin voice was cold, distant, as if it'd been raked over coals and dragged back again. "Are you finished?" he rasped, drawing the whiskey bottle to his lips and taking a generous sip.

Kharis waved a dismissive hand toward him.

"It was an error in judgement."

"An error in judgement?" Kharis scoffed, still pacing. "You might as well have handed all our heads over to Lucien on a plate. Fucking error in judgement my arse. *If* we survive this, we'll be dealing with the repercussions of this for years. Decades!" he hissed.

"I said, are you fucking finished yet, Kharis, so that I might speak?" Corbin muttered from where he lay.

Kharis growled at him, only daring to do so because they were friends, because he'd earned that right over the years. Through loyalty and good judgement.

Traits which Corbin apparently had very little of.

"You were right," he said, calmly, his hate aimed only at himself and himself alone. "I made a mistake. But she can still prove useful. We can—"

"Do you even hear yourself?" Kharis sneered as he shook his head in disbelief. "You just single-handedly ensured Lucien continues to haunt us, if he doesn't manage to kill us all first, and all you can think about is a bit of human cunt?"

Even Corbin was surprised at how fast he moved, his hand clutching Kharis' throat in an instant. "I told you never to speak of her that way again."

"Did you?" Kharis lifted a brow, unfazed.

With a rough shove, Corbin released him, pacing the length of the room, whiskey bottle still in hand. He hadn't bothered to change out of his blood covered shirt, the unbuttoned material still littered with bullet wounds, though his body had rejected the blasted things hours ago.

It took more than a handful of bullets to kill an ancient vampire, that much was true. Only a stake to the heart or decapitation brought his kind to an end. As he'd asked his men to do with every associate of Lucien's who'd been in that room.

"Turn her and let's be done with this. Once and for all," Kharis said.

It was the logical solution, the sensible solution, and yet...

"I can't."

"What in flying fuck do you mean you can't?" Kharis snarled. "You can't be serious, Corbin. It's been years. Centuries, even. You cannot mean to tell me you're still afraid of—"

"The only thing which fills me with fear is the thought of more human blood on my hands." Corbin glared over his shoulder at his friend. "She stays human."

"God fucking damnit," Kharis whispered, watching as Corbin turned toward him. Shaking his head, Kharis started laughing then, humorless chuckles, his face unamused. "You right piece of shit, I don't know how I didn't see it before."

Corbin looked toward him.

"You love her, don't you?" The ancient Greek lifted a brow.

Corbin scoffed. "Don't be ridiculous, Kharis. I—"

"Oh, shut up, Corbin, before you make yourself even more of a fool." Kharis scowled, finally stepping away from the wall. "You've been saving Dani for years. Don't tell me you haven't realized it?"

Corbin stayed silent for a long beat, for once, uncertain what to do.

As he'd been the moment she'd pulled that skeleton key from round her neck.

He was a vampire. He wasn't capable of love. He shouldn't be, and yet...

"Good God, man," Kharis swore, raking a hand over his face, "you really are fucked in the head, aren't you?"

Corbin couldn't bring himself to look at Kharis. "I'm handling it."

"Are you?" Kharis shouted, ripping the whiskey bottle from Corbin's hand and throwing it against the drywall. The bottle smashed upon impact, the contents and broken glass scattering across the floor. "Well, fucking handle it better, because from where I sit, unless you do, you're about to lose *everything* that matters to that monster that fucking sired you, unless..." Kharis' gaze swept over him, his eyes going wide in horror, like he'd never seen him before. "Unless this is what you wanted, didn't you? Unless you did this as some fucked penance to punish yourself for what happened to Ros—"

"Do not speak her name in my presence, do you hear me?" Corbin sneered. "You're not worthy of it."

"And neither are you," Kharis yelled, stabbing a finger against Corbin's chest. "Then or now. Nor do you deserve that poor woman in there." He gestured wildly in the direction of Corbin's living room, where Dani no doubt waited.

Corbin's face remained still, even as his undead pulse beat. He'd expected her to leave, to place distance between them, never wish to see him again, like she was *supposed* to do, though Dani never had made choices in her own best interest, had she?

"Yes, she stayed," Kharis answered his question, before

Corbin even had a chance to ask it. "Somehow, you haven't managed to chase her away just yet. I was as surprised as you." Kharis stepped forward then, gripping Corbin by the back of the neck, and pressing their foreheads together as they used to on the streets.

Brother to brother.

"You don't get to decide what gifts life gives and takes away from you. You only get to decide your actions, what you do, and so help me God, brother, you best decide soon, because until then, my job here is through."

Abruptly, Kharis released him, stalking toward the door.

"You don't fucking mean that," Corbin called after him.

"Like hell I don't!" Kharis shot over his shoulder, still angry. Rightfully so.

And then Kharis was gone, leaving Corbin alone in his thoughts, to stew on his mistakes once more. Which served exactly as the kind of punishment Kharis had intended it to.

DANI SAT on the sofa in Corbin's living room, glaring out at the darkened night, the Chicago skyline illuminating the shadows of the city below. She'd sat here for hours, waiting for who or for what she never knew. Perhaps sunrise, or maybe, her own death considering Lucien was still on the run, whichever came first. It wasn't as if she had anywhere else to go, anyone else to run to. Save to her brother, of course. But when was the last time Quinn had helped her?

He'd likely just tell her what an idiot she was, because once again, she'd allowed herself to be fooled, because that's what vampires did, didn't they?

They fucked you.

In more ways than one.

Corbin included.

Dani's hair was still damp, the strands dripping about her shoulders from where one of Corbin's men had deposited her in the shower upon their return. Fully clothed and weeping, she'd lain there sobbing for long enough that the water running over her bloodstained clothes and body had run clean, until finally, she'd managed to peel herself off the shower floor, and pulled herself together. Because that's what Dani did best.

She survived. She endured. Whatever life threw at her.

No matter how fucked and twisted.

And this about topped the levels of fucked, even by her measures.

She shifted her weight, adjusting herself where she sat, naked save for one of Corbin's shirts she wore. It smelled like him. Like frankincense, orange, and cedarwood. All things that'd once been a comfort to her. That were *still* a comfort to her, no matter how much she didn't want it to be true. What would he have to do to her for her to want to leave?

Dani wasn't certain she knew the answer.

She was still mulling that over when Corbin finally decided to join her in the living room, looking as alive and well as ever, despite his blood-soaked, open shirt, and unkempt hair.

That's what the undead do, she thought to herself. *Survive. Only to fuck you once more.*

They always lived to see another day, no matter how horrible they were to one another. Now that he was truly dead, even Cillian still lived on in the ghostly memories that haunted her.

But what else was new?

No one had ever said life was fair, and Dani had known

that from a very young age. From the first time someone had fucked her like this.

"I suppose you thought, 'what could it hurt'?" she whispered, breaking the pressing silence between them. "What could it hurt for poor, pathetic Dani to be fucked one more time?" She lifted her gaze toward him, repeating the same question that'd been on her lips before. "How could you?"

Corbin refused to look toward her. "It wasn't about you."

"Oh, it wasn't?" She lifted a sarcastic brow. "Then exactly *who* was it about when you lied to me, Corbin? When you told me there was nothing in it for you? When you tried to claim my revenge as your own? I thought you were doing me a favor."

"I was." He finally looked toward her then. "You want Lucien dead, too. Don't deny it."

SHE SHOOK HER HEAD. "That's not what we agreed."

She'd planned her revenge and killing Lucien hadn't been a part of it.

Only seeing him locked up for an eternity would do. Caged like the animal he was.

Unable to escape the consequences of his actions, like *she* was unable to escape the memories of him hurting her.

Or so she'd thought, until tonight.

Facing him had been enough, until the bullets had flown.

And then she had realized Corbin was right. She wanted Lucien dead too, but that didn't excuse the way he'd lied to her. What kind of woman did that make her?

"You lied to me," she hissed, doubling down. It didn't matter that he was right, that she wanted Lucien dead as much as he did. She should have been informed.

Corbin's expression hardened. "You were offered everything you asked for in exchange for attending a party, nothing more. I apologize if that was a chore for you."

From the smug look on Corbin's face, he knew that it wasn't.

Heat flooded her cheeks. Shame, too.

What do you expect when you literally begged him to touch you? she chastised herself.

How could she have been such a fool?

"There was never any journal, was there? That was all part of the lie too."

Corbin didn't answer, he simply watched her, his expression as unmoving as a statue.

"And now, I suppose you expect me to say thank you for nearly getting me killed?"

Corbin scoffed. "Nearly is a matter of semantics and dramatics, darling. You could *nearly* die at any moment. It's part of being human, yet here you stand, living and breathing among the undead, don't you?"

"And I suppose I should be thanking you for that too?" She sneered.

Corbin returned the look. "You were *supposed* to be safely upstairs. Had you been injured you would have been collateral damage. It wasn't personal."

"And that's supposed to make it better?" she shouted at him, jaw clenching. "I don't know what to do with you." She waved her hands as if she were prepared to storm off, though she didn't know where to. Not with Lucien still at large.

"It's simple, Dani. As I've told you dozens of times before." Corbin stepped forward, pegging her with a hardened stare. "Leave, and don't come back to this world," his gaze raked over her, hot and wanting, the next words he spoke new, "or else I'll ruin you too."

She dropped her hands to her sides, exasperated. "What does that even mean?"

"Already I see the ways this world, the ways *I* have changed you." Corbin's glare was like diamonds then, so intense and sharp it could cut. "It means that if you had even an ounce of fucking self-preservation you wouldn't parade yourself before me the way you do."

"So now it's my fault?" Dani's jaw dropped. "Not you too. Now you sound just like my brother, trying to make my decisions for me."

"At least he has the goddamn bloody sense not to risk himself!"

"Fuck you!" she shouted at him, drawing so close to his face, she could practically breathe him in, though she hadn't planned to. "Fuck you and the horse you rode in on, Corbin. The only fault here is with you." She stabbed one slender finger into the stone wall of his chest, causing him to snarl at her. "You never once questioned why I kept coming back, did you? Why I would never take the goddamn hint and leave?"

Stalking past her, Corbin wrenched open the penthouse door, attempting to wave her through it. "I have little use for you now, human. Leave, before I change my mind."

"You really don't realize, do you?" She stared at him, incredulously. "All this time, all this risk I've placed myself in. You've never once realized it's all been for you. In a desperate, ridiculous search for your attention, all in hope that one day you'd finally notice, and—"

"I *have* noticed you, Dani," Corbin hissed, stopping her short. "I do nothing *but* notice you."

Dani's breath caught, her stupid, foolish heart hammering away inside her chest.

"Every time you walk into a room, every smile you gift to another. I've noticed. All of it." Corbin looked toward her then, his eyes meeting hers.

"And yet, it meant nothing to you?" she whispered. "Am I that undesirable?"

"You are many things, Dani," Corbin shook his head, easing toward her, "but undesirable isn't one of them." He prowled toward her then, his stride languid, his steps true. "What would you have me do?" he whispered, his voice velvet and smooth, a seductive touch against skin. "Keep you, turn you? Is that what you want?" He held her face in his hand once more. "I haven't even fucked you, Dani, and already you have me wrapped around your finger." The tortured look in his eyes tore through her. "What else would you have me do?"

She fell silent then, uncertain what to say. "So, you'd rather say goodbye before ever even giving us a real chance? Leave me alone to die like I meant nothing to you?" She shook her head, pulling away a little. "Like you said, we haven't even fucked."

"Does that matter?" Corbin asked, his gaze piercing through her. "Do you want to?"

Dani crossed her arms over her chest, refusing to look at him.

But she could feel his gaze on her, hot and searing.

"Is that what it'll take to convince you to save yourself from all the ways I am unable to protect you?"

Her eyes shot toward him then.

She'd never once considered that the danger she placed herself in might affect him to, might...concern him.

"You *do* want that, don't you, Dani? And that thrills you."

He eased closer, gripping her flush against him, so that she could feel the hardened length of his cock against her. "Is that what you want, Dani? To fuck a monster?"

"You're not a monster, Corbin." She shook her head a little. "No matter what Lucien has done to you."

He laughed then, dark and wicked. "Foolish, foolish, girl."

Before Dani even knew what he was doing, he was holding her by her throat once more, making it difficult to breathe.

"I am a monster," Corbin whispered, the heat of his breath tracing over her chin, "the kind which preys upon innocents like you." His tongue ran over his teeth then, his fangs lengthening. "A shame you weren't smart enough to see it."

His grip on her loosened, and Dani stumbled back slightly, her base instincts getting the better of her.

Corbin chuckled, fangs flashing. "Don't bother to run, Dani. It'll only make things worse if you do." His dark stare pierced through her. "Because if you run, I *will* chase you, and I *will* find you, and then I shan't be held accountable for what happens next."

Dani shuddered, before instantly going still.

"Are you scared now?" he whispered, crimson eyes staring at her.

She really *was* a fool, but she supposed she always had been. For him, at least.

She shook her head a little. "No."

"Pity." Corbin stepped toward her, stroking one slow languid hand over her the exposed skin at her collar. "You've no idea what I'm about to do."

Dani bristled. She wasn't some virgin to this, untried and new. "I've been bitten before."

"Oh, darling." He chuckled. "Not like this."

Corbin moved so fast she didn't even see him throw back his head, his strike on her neck swift and fierce, filled with all the venom of a poisonous snake.

But it wasn't poison she felt course through her.

It was desire. Pure, and raw, and lustful.

More intense than any bodily experience she'd ever known.

She was coming in an instant, finding release, and still begging for more.

More.

More. More. More.

Pleasure the likes of which she'd never known coursed through her. She was hot, wanton with need. It was enough she nearly lost herself to it, enough she would have been happy to stay right there, locked in his arms for eternity, for the rest of forever, even as she felt herself grow weak, even as she felt herself grow cold.

Dani teetered on the edge of consciousness, ready and willing to slip into the dark, until suddenly Corbin pulled back, releasing her, slamming her back into reality.

Dani blinked, coming to senses, for once truly frightened.

Because unlike when Cillian and Lucien had hurt her, she hadn't been drugged, hadn't been filled with fear. She'd seen the Angel of Death and welcomed him with open arms.

And she couldn't find two fucks to give.

"*La petite mort,*" Corbin whispered against her ear, whilst still lapping her blood from his lips. "It's French, and modern scholars will tell you it means this," Corbin's hand dove beneath his shirt which she wore, roughly parting her legs and finding her clit, instantly causing her to come once more. She shuddered against him, ecstasy barreling through her.

His bite was orgasmic, and she was still high from the sensation of it. She'd never be able to finish like this on her own.

"But in truth, the phrase is far older, and it means to this," he laid a soft kiss at her throat, the spot where he'd marked her, bitten her. "A vampire's kiss. A little death."

His tongue circled each small puncture, sealing it closed as she let out a pleasured groan, his mark still apparent.

"The true question is, Dani," he pulled her close, claiming her lips in a soft, tender kiss, as he whispered, "How much do you want to die?"

8

For once, Corbin didn't stop to consider the repercussions of what he was doing, didn't pause to plan or calculate. All he wanted was to bury himself inside Dani, to wring another orgasm from between those silky lips. Consequences be damned. He'd tried his damnedest to resist her before, but now, in the face of all he'd lost for her, he couldn't help himself.

Corbin lifted her into his arms, moving with supernatural grace and speed, as he deposited her onto his bed, his hands working in a fury. He had her naked before him in an instant, tearing his own shirt to shreds, and leaving Dani spread eagle and bare before him, save for that goddamn necklace key.

Corbin reached down, gripping the old skeleton key in his fist. "How long?" he whispered. "How long have you had this?"

"A few years," Dani shrugged, unknowingly, wiggling closer to the edge of the bed near him. "Someone left it for me at the Midnight Coyote."

Blood fire sparked in his eyes then, his lust going feral. "And you've held onto it since?"

She nodded. "It...it came with a note. From a friend, or so, it said." She shrugged a little, half-lidded eyes looking at him. "They didn't leave a name. I always figured it was one of the regulars. Someone who admired me a bit."

Corbin growled his disapproval. "And do you remember what the note said?"

Dani smiled a little, reclaiming it from his hands as if she were holding a precious gift. "It said that the key to all my desires was within my reach, if only I knew where to look for it."

"And did you?" he asked, his attention rapt, eyes combing her face, her breasts, each breath. "Did you know where to look for it, Dani?"

She shrugged once more like she wasn't certain why it mattered to him. "I don't know. I always sort of assumed it was just a message to me, encouragement to claim my power, to not be under Cillian's thumb anymore. It made me feel like I could be brave."

"And that's why you kept it?" he asked, bending to lay a kiss on one of her breasts. His tongue darted over one peaked nipple.

"Yes," she breathed, arching into him. "Yes, it reminds me I have a choice, a say in where my life goes."

Corbin didn't breathe. "And the key?" he asked. "Do you know what it opens?"

Her brow furrowed a little like she was confused by his question. "I...I never bothered to try it, I guess. I wouldn't know where to look."

Corbin swallowed, his emotions thick in his throat. "A shame," he said, lowering himself over her. "After all, keys are meant to open doors, and open doors lead to new opportunities." He dropped to his knees before her, spreading her wide as he teased her pussy with one slow lick. "What opportunity did you miss, Dani?"

Dani moaned, her answer lost to the heat of his mouth swallowing her whole. His tongue circled her clit, giving and taking. It didn't take long, until she was bucking against him, coming against his mouth. She was still riding high from his bite, and he hadn't even given her a drink of him yet.

"So responsive, so soft," he whispered against her as she shivered.

Corbin stood then, shucking off his clothes and allowing them to fall to the floor, until he stood naked before her, his cock hard and ready.

"You're beautiful," she whispered, her tongue darting out to wet her lips, like she was hungry from him. Her gaze raked over his nude form and settled on the bead of moisture at the tip of his cock. He smirked at her, tsking his tongue a little.

She didn't know hunger, and she never would. Not like he did.

Not the kind of hunger that could consume until there was little room left for anything else to exist. He didn't wish even upon his worst enemy, not even Lucien.

"No more beautiful than you, darling," he said, drinking her in. "You're exquisite."

He took one of her breasts into his mouth, gently pinching and playing with it, until she was gasping, begging for more. Her hands twisted into his hair.

"May I enter you?" he whispered against her skin. "Make you mine?"

"Yes," she panted. "Yes, I might die if you don't."

Corbin chuckled. "Oh, Dani. You have no idea how close

to death you humans really are." He flipped her over then, entering her pussy from behind on a heated thrust. Dani cried out, throwing her head back with the pleasure of it.

Moving them once more, Corbin gripped hold of her hair, arching her back until she was nearly riding him whilst standing, his other hand in control of her hips. Dani's hands fell to her breasts, clutching and kneading greedily, as she took her pleasure.

"Say you're mine," Corbin whispered against her throat. "I wish to hear it."

"I'm yours," Dani panted.

He tugged her hair, arching her back further. "Louder."

"I'm yours!" Dani practically shouted.

Anything to please him.

"Good girl," he praised her. "Now, stay still for a bit."

Corbin bit into her, thrusting in time along with it. His mouth sucking, and his cock pumping until both of them were nearly crazed with it.

"Come for me, Dani," he hissed, releasing her from his blood-stained lips. "Come for me and tell me this was never just for show."

"It isn't," she cried. "It wasn't."

"It was real," he admitted. "It was real for us both."

Dani cried out then, clenching around him for several thrusts until a moment later, he spent himself in her, his cum trickling down her legs, same as the blood which coated her throat.

He laid her down on the bed then, drawing her against him as he sealed her wounds.

Fuck, she was beautiful, far more delicate and fragile than he'd ever envisioned, her pulse fluttering like a butterfly he could crush in his hands.

"What happens now, Dani? What happens after this?"

She didn't answer him for a long time, instead choosing only to cuddle against him. Until finally, she rose. "You owe me a blood oath," she said, climbing on top of him to straddle his hips. She offered him her wrist then, allowing him to bite her there once more. Eagerly, he sucked from her, greedy, harsh pulls that made him hard in an instant, ready for her again.

Pulling back her wrist once more, she sank down onto his cock with a delicious, throaty groan. "A blood oath that says the next time you take your revenge against Lucien, that *we* shall share it, that his life will be mine to claim alongside you and yours, and that you will never lie to me again." She lifted herself up, swirling her hips, teasing him with whether she would sink down and put him out of his misery. "No more lies. No more secrets."

He could be inside her for centuries and never tire of it.

But they only had a few decades more, at most.

"Swear it," she whispered harshly. Pure harpy once more. "Swear it and I'm forever yours."

Corbin chuckled, shaking his head. What could a human possibly know of forever?

But damn it, if she didn't already have him wrapped around her finger already.

"You have my word," he swore, bringing his wrist to his lips.

He bit down, drawing blood before offering it to her, encouraging her to drink. "What's mine is yours, darling," he said, lifting his wrist to her lips, "and what's yours is mine."

Dani placed her mouth on his wrist, tasting him as he had her.

"Drink deep," he growled, and to his satisfaction, she did.

CORBIN LAY AWAKE LONG into the midnight hours, until it became sunrise and then dusk again, his body unmoving, whilst Dani lay tucked into his side, sleeping. Time often passed for him in a blur like this. Little more than a brief flash of memory, the years speeding by with ever-increasing speed. Eternity was truly endless.

Eventually, he rose, padding naked from his room and down the abandoned penthouse corridor. Only to find Kharis alone, smoking a cigarette in his living room.

"So, you fucked her."

His friend didn't say anything more, before Corbin sat across from him on the sofa, nicking one of his cigarettes from the open box upon the table. He grabbed Kharis' lighter, the one he'd given him several holidays ago as a gift, flicking it open and lighting up, before he took a long drag of his own.

"Did you turn her?" Kharis asked.

"No." Corbin leaned forward, flicking his ashes into a waiting crystal dish. "No, not yet."

"Mmm," Kharis hummed. "Is the delay for her benefit or for yours?"

Corbin crossed his legs, leaning his arms back onto the couch as he took a long drag in answer.

"If that's how it's to be, I suppose." Kharis stubbed his cigarette butt into the waiting tray. "Lucien's already reached out to his other contacts. To the Morettis and Tedescos, hoping they'll back him."

Corbin lifted a brow, blowing out smoke. "And will they?"

"That remains to be seen." Kharis leaned back, looking

at him once more. "This is bad, Corbin. As bad as it's ever been."

Corbin nodded. "I know."

"And was it worth it? Choosing her over your own?"

Corbin stubbed out the remainder of his cigarette and rose. "Ask me in a few days' time."

"You still truly believe you can pull this off, don't you?" Kharis said over his shoulder.

"That you can somehow find a way out of this?"

"There's always a way, Kharis. There's always a way for men who are desperate." Corbin paused.

"That's the problem. Based on the last few hours, I'm not certain you're desperate *enough*," Kharis spat.

Corbin's voice remained as calm as it was cold. "Lucien has already taken everything from me once before," he said. "I won't allow him to do so again."

Corbin returned to his room then, leaving Kharis alone to sulk.

Dani was just rousing from her sleep as he entered.

"Corbin?" she whispered through the dark, blue eyes searching.

"Right here, darling. I didn't leave you for long."

He joined her in his bed then, pulling her against him. In a single night, they'd made love nearly a dozen times or more, and still, he wasn't satiated, wasn't satisfied.

When would it be enough?

He traced his hand over the smooth skin of her neck, the puncture wounds he'd left there.

"What shall I do now, Dani?" he mused. "What would you have me do?"

"Turn me," she whispered, confirming his greatest fear. "Turn me. Make me well and truly yours."

Corbin couldn't bring himself to move. "I can't," he breathed. "Forgive me, darling, but I won't."

She twisted toward him then, staring up at him through the dark as if his expression contained all the world's greatest mysteries, until finally, she whispered, "I understand." The hurt in her eyes killed him a little. It was like she was destroying him from the inside out.

Bit by bit. Piece by piece.

She sat up, moving to the edge of the bed. "And what of Lucien? What of him?"

"I made you a promise, and I intend to keep it."

She nodded, temporarily appeased. "And your plan?"

Corbin huffed, leaning back against the pillows. "Hell if I know, luv."

"Good," Dani said, instantly drawing his gaze again. "Good, because I do."

Corbin sat up, moving across the bed to prop himself on his elbow as he kissed along the skin of her arm, her shoulder. "And what pray tell, do you propose?" he whispered.

"I've had my revenge, but now it's time for me to help you get yours." Dani stood from the bed, pulling away from him suddenly in a way that caused him to hiss in protest. "I think we may need to call my brother."

9

"**T**he fate of our entire organization depends on this meeting. Do *not* fuck this up."

"I believe we heard you the first several times you said it, Kharis. Must it bear repeating once more?" Corbin rolled his eyes again.

"He's concerned for you, that's all," Dani said, glancing down at her nails as if to examine their polish. They were sitting in Corbin's living room, waiting on Quinn's arrival.

Kharis scoffed. "You credit me with far too much emotion, human."

"Do I?" Dani blinked, turning innocent-doe eyes toward Kharis. "Or are you simply not brave enough to admit to it?"

Kharis growled, looking toward Corbin. "Are you certain you want to keep her?" he hissed. "She seems to have a sharp mouth."

"I rather like her mouth," Corbin said, waving a hand in dismissal as he beckoned Dani onto his lap. "And if you weren't too busy sulking over the fact that she sees right through you, I think you would too."

"Fools." Kharis scowled. "The both of you. This isn't going to work."

Dani batted her eyes at him. "Not with that attitude it won't."

A knock sounded at the door then, drawing all their attention.

A moment later, Quinn strode in, his already frowning face pulling into a scowl the moment he spotted Dani in Corbin's lap. "I suppose I shouldn't be surprised," he said, his Stetson barely hiding his derisive sneer. It was the closest he'd ever come to looking as if he were disgusted with her, but Dani couldn't bring herself to care anymore.

She was done being the plaything of powerful men.

Corbin included.

And when this business was through, she'd claim her own destiny.

Even if she had to walk away and never come back.

She'd decided upon it the moment Corbin had said he wouldn't turn her.

That he wouldn't offer her the kind of power that had been gifted to him.

Dani wasn't perfect. She had little illusion of that. She was often mild and meek and too willing to let others take control, to make decisions for her, because she'd spent the whole of her life like that, trapped between the wills of powerful men. First her brother, countless boyfriends, and then Cillian—and now, Corbin—he may have wanted her, but he too refused to share his power with her, to make her immortal, to finally give her the means to protect herself, though she'd been robbed of the instinct from the start of her early years.

And how *exactly* was that her fault?

Her life, her choices were a result of a trauma response, plain and simple.

And now, she had the chance to truly stand up for herself for the first time in years.

To start anew. To be reborn.

She wouldn't let *anyone* take it away from her.

Not even Corbin. Even if it meant she had to double cross him, as he had her.

Revenge was a cyclical thing, or so she was discovering.

"Thank you for joining us, Quinn," she said, her voice dripping with venom, "since it was your idea that I return to this world in the first place."

If her brother was going to look down his nose at her and her choices, she planned to remind him of the role he'd played in getting her here at every opportunity she got.

At that, Quinn seemed to hesitate a little, tipping his Stetson as if he were giving in. "You've made your point, Dani," he drawled. "Now explain to me what I'm doing here."

"We need your help," she said, using his own words against him. "The *Cosa della notte* syndicate that is."

Beside her, Kharis sputtered on his drink. If Corbin's underboss had expected he knew how this meeting would go, this clearly wasn't it.

Corbin, on the other hand, didn't so much as flinch.

"I'm listening," Quinn said, urging her to go on.

Dani held her head high, going in for the kill. "We need the Execution Underground's resources, if you expect us to hand over Lucien, that is."

"Us?" Quinn echoed.

"Yes, *us*," Dani said, feeling more than seeing the prideful smirk that undoubtedly pulled at Corbin's lips.

"That's how exchanges work, you see. They go both ways. You get what you want and so do we."

Quinn scowled. "And what exactly is it you want?"

"Immunity," she said, trying and failing to ignore the way Corbin's cock had grown stiff against her bottom, his desire for her seeming to increase with every word. "For the next ten years or more, you leave the syndicate alone."

Quinn laughed then, placing his hands on his hips as he shook his head. "And why the hell would we make a deal like that?"

"Because we're not just going to give you Lucien," she said, preparing to deliver the final blow. "We'll give you every other boss in the syndicate, so long as you leave Corbin in charge."😊

∾

"I DON'T LIKE THIS. I don't like this one bit."

"No one ever asked for your approval, Kharis, only for your cooperation."

Corbin stepped inside the empty church, his steps falling heavy on the cathedral's marble flooring. The darkened rafters of the vaulted ceiling loomed over them, the backlit lights of the city illuminating the colors of the several stained-glass windows within view.

It wasn't as if vampires couldn't stand upon consecrated ground, but somehow, since his own death, Corbin always found the atmosphere of churches and religion to be quite eerie.

"Cooperation?" To his left, Kharis scoffed. "*You* of all vampires truly feel as if you're in a place to demand that?"

"He has a point," Dani answered, squeezing where she held his hand a little.

Corbin rolled his eyes at Kharis in dismissal. "What's that phrase you Americans say?" Corbin asked, glancing toward her. "Go big or go home?"

"In this case, 'going big' means risking our bloody necks," Kharis hissed, his voice echoing through the candlelit dark.

Corbin sighed for what felt like the thousandth time this evening. "You've already lived several hundred years, Kharis. If tonight is truly the end, you hardly have place to complain."

Kharis muttered something fowl under his breath, striding further into the church as he shook his head, murmuring something or other about the pitfalls of loyalty, until Corbin and Dani were left standing there alone, holding hands in the church's main aisle.

Corbin stared up at the stained-glass window just below the altar ceiling overhead.

"Were you Catholic?" Dani asked softly, breaking the silence between them. "Before you were turned, that is?"

Corbin took a moment to consider, before he answered, "Yes. Or something like it." He looked toward her.

In the flickering glow of the church candles, she was so beautiful it almost pained him.

Perfect and flawed. A match for him in every way.

"And you?" he asked.

Dani lifted a brow.

"Were you Catholic before, before you learned about our world I mean?" he elaborated.

Dani smiled then, glancing up at the altar's wooden crucifix, before glancing down to where she nervously shuffled her feet. A poor attempt to hide the blush in her cheeks. "Considering my reputation, do you even have to ask, Corbin?"

Corbin blinked, surprised and more than a little taken aback, before an unexpected bark of laughter tore from his throat. "Is that a schoolgirl joke?"

Dani didn't respond, simply smiled coyly, shrugging her slender shoulders a little, before leaving him to take her seat in the front row pew.

That was what he loved about her most, that she was constantly surprising him.

Making him feel. Making him remember the man he was.

Or had once been long ago.

Every time he thought he'd learned Dani's truth, there was one layer, one other part of her that he had not seen. One part of him that she had not touched, hadn't awoken what had been missing. What endless gifts might he unlock? What pleasures if they had an eternity?

But there was no eternity for her, and there never would be.

No, he may have been too selfish to have let her go, but that didn't mean he wouldn't encourage her to live her life, and live it well, before she grew old and passed peacefully in her sleep. How could what he offered her be better?

Even if *this* was what she chose. Or wanted to choose for herself. This undead existence he was living. He'd love her for eternity, that much was true, but eternity to a human....

She didn't know understand the true meaning.

How could he ask that of her and more?

Corbin lingered where he stood for a long time, torn between joining her and Kharis, or allowing himself this space, this moment to grieve. He hadn't been inside a church in several centuries, since not long after Rosalind had died.

He'd need to tell Dani about her soon, considering the promises he'd made.

"You know what I still don't understand," Kharis finally said, twisting from where he sat in one of the front pews, "how did Lucien know to glamour that poor woman?"

"Someone tipped him off in advance, clearly." Dani shook her head in disappointment.

Corbin had known it, too

He had suspected the botched attempt on Lucien's life was *entirely* his fault.

"But who?" Dani asked, just as the old wooden door to the church opened and closed, a sharp click of high heels following in its wake.

"Cassandra," Corbin answered, uttering her name by way of greeting as the siren entered the room.

Cassandra was breathtaking, of course. All sirens were great beauties. With flowing hair and bright eyes and curves that could stretch for days. But all Corbin saw now when he looked at her was disloyalty, hatred, greed. Greed that he would not gift her his heart, although he'd tried thoroughly.

Unfortunately, it'd already been claimed by another.

Though he hadn't yet realized.

His gaze fell to Dani, the way her eyes went wide and how the point of her chin quivered briefly as she took in Cassandra's beauty. But there was no comparison between them. Cassandra was perfect, unflawed, as angelic as she was deadly, and Dani, well, her flaws only enhanced her beauty, only made her truer, more real, and lovely.

Crafted by the hand of God in every way.

He looked toward Cassandra once more. He'd known she'd be sour that he'd chosen to end things between them, but he hadn't exactly expected for her to sell him out either.

Clearly, Corbin had a blind spot when it came to the women in his life.

Kharis had been telling him as much for centuries.

"Kharis," Cassandra said, pointedly greeting his friend first, before finally turning her glowing violet eyes toward him. "Corbin," she said, almost affectionately, her gaze raking over him, "You look like shit." She strode past him then, no longer bothering with false pretense.

And that was Cassandra essentially.

A fierce beauty, and an even fiercer bitch.

Hands still in his pockets, Corbin twisted, his gaze following her as she went. He released an exasperated sigh. "Hello to you, too, Cassandra."

Cassandra strode right down the aisle, hips swaying as if she were practically cat-walking, before she stopped a few rows a way from Dani, tilting her head curiously. "So, you're the new mistress?"

"New?" Dani blinked, quickly glancing between them. "I...wasn't aware anyone else had filled the position."

Cassandra shrugged. "Don't be too precious about it." She waved a manicured hand in dismissal, plopping down in the nearest pew seat, before adjusting the strap on one of her Jimmy Choos. "He'll get rid of you too. Just give it time. He does it with all of us."

"Cassandra," Corbin growled in warning.

"What?" Cassandra asked, glaring at him expectantly. "It's true. He's still hung up on some hum—" The siren paused for a moment, inhaling as if she were a bloodhound who'd just caught a sudden, unexplained scent on the wind. Slowly, she twisted back toward Dani then, eyes filled with hatred anew. "Oh, it's you." She shot a harsh glare toward Corbin. "Finally got around to fucking her, did you? Tell me, did she let you feed from her thigh while she blew you in sixty-nine?" Her eyes shot to Dani. "He likes that a lot."

"*Enough*, Cassandra," Corbin snarled.

"Or what?" she challenged. "You'll put out a hit on me, too?" She arched one sculpted brow, before making a show of checking her manicure. "Lucien wasn't too pleased about that."

This time, it was Kharis' turn to speak. "You're lucky I don't gut you from your cunt to your ears, you traitorous sow."

"Language, Kharis," Cassandra tsked, chastising him as if he were a child. "After all, there's a human here." Her gaze fell pointedly toward Dani, before flicking back to Corbin. "They're such weak creatures, as you know."

Corbin had to force himself to swallow the growl that rumbled in his throat. He had known he'd regret the day he told Cassandra about Rosalind, about the children, especially now that he hadn't yet confided the same to Dani, but he hadn't expected that regret to bite him for another several years, at least.

Apparently, sirens made their vengeance quick.

"No matter," Cassandra said, waving her hand dismissively.

Had she always put on this much of a show? Corbin's scowl deepened slightly.

"We're here as friends now," Cassandra continued, smiling devilishly, "after all, Angelo brought me here."

"Of course he did," Corbin snapped. "Angelo was always pleased to dine on someone else's leftovers."

"Leftovers, hmm?" Cassandra said, eyes narrowing. "And what about you, human?" Cassandra said, turning her attention toward Dani once more. "How does it feel to enjoy the leftovers of a dead woman?"

Dani blinked. "Excuse me?"

"I said, *enough*, Cassandra!" Corbin roared, his voice echoing throughout the cathedral.

"What? Did I say something wrong?" Cassandra placed a hand to her chest, batting her long eyelashes innocently. "You mean to tell me she didn't know you had a wife and children?"

"With you?" Dani asked suddenly, her eyes nearly popping from her head.

Cassandra wrinkled her nose. "Oh, no. I'd never destroy my body that way. He—"

Corbin's voice grew low and cold. "So, help me, God. Cassandra, if you utter one more word—"

"You'll what?" Angelo asked, finally joining them. "You wouldn't want this little meeting of yours to start off on the wrong foot now would you, Corbin?"

"Angelo," Corbin muttered his greeting through clenched teeth.

Angelo preened. "I see Cassandra's told you she's found herself a new family as of late."

Corbin sneered. "My deepest felicitations, I assure you."

For several minutes, they were then forced to wait in silence as Cassandra and Angelo put on their little show, the traitorous siren sitting in Angelo's lap, covering his face in overly sugary kisses and whispering sweet nothings that, had she been watching, would have made even the statue of the Virgin Mary which overlooked them blush like a whore.

Corbin rubbed his temples, already far too close to losing his patience, before the meeting had even begun, until finally their other guests arrived. Roman, Salvatore, and Mickey, Lucien's closest ranked representative, filed in, taking their respective seats spread out among the pews.

Corbin's hit had taken out several of Lucien's men ranked over him.

"Well, best get on with it," Angelo grumbled from where Cassandra still peppered kisses across his face, nuzzling into Angelo's neck.

It wasn't as if Corbin felt any hint of jealousy toward them. In fact, if Cassandra hadn't turned out to be such a traitorous snake all because he'd chosen to end them, he would have gladly wished her the best, perhaps even been *happy* for her and Angelo, as disgusting as he found their blatant display of tomfoolery to be. He may have been a willing participant in public sex, but that had been inside his own club, not on a goddamn church pulpit, though the idea *did* hold a certain appeal, if he was honest.

No, instead what concerned him was how silent Dani had been.

How quiet and mild and meek. As she'd always expected her to be before.

Except he'd seen a change in her over these past few days, hadn't he?

Something that hinted at the true woman beneath.

But there wasn't time to ask about that now, to tend whatever wounds Cassandra's presence had opened. Instead, there was business. The plan which they'd built together.

Corbin cleared his throat, stepping forward. "I'm sure you're all eager to know why I've summoned you here, and so shortly after Lucien's near death." He nodded to Mickey, who did little more than curl a lip at him menacingly. The Irishman would be lucky to breathe another breath when this was through, but Corbin continued, ignoring him.

"Best get on with it now, Corbin. We haven't got all night." This from Angelo, of course. Ever hurried.

"We're vampires. We have an eternity," Corbin answered. "But apparently, that isn't long enough to teach you the concept of patience, is it, Angelo?"

Kharis and a few of the others chuckled, causing Angelo to seethe, whilst Cassandra practically licked his nonexistent wounds. It was disgusting really.

Corbin turned his attention back toward the room. "It recently occurred to me that we haven't all come together like this in years," he said, pointedly looking toward them. "And thus, I have a proposal to make." He placed his hands in his pockets, glancing down at his feet, before he began circling, working the room as he had countless times before. "Any man, vampire, or woman in this room, who has an interest in what I'm about to say is welcome to stay."

He paused, dramatically. "Anyone else is free to take their leave."

A wooden scrape of more than one pew bench followed, Roman and Mickey, moving to leave. As he'd suspected.

"But be apprised that if and when you walk through those doors," he said, speaking after them, causing them to pause, "there will be a legion of human hunters waiting to greet you as you do."

Immediately, shouts went up as the other vampires rounded on him, their bloody curses and furious hissing echoing off the cathedral ceiling.

Kharis fired a round into the rafters, a chunk of granite raining down. "Quiet," he barked.

Corbin lifted a hand in agreement, silencing every person in the room, before he continued. "However, should you like to leave here today without the true death greeting you at the exit door, there is a choice to be made." Slowly, he looked to each one of them. "Join me, and my crew, *without* stepping down from your respective positions and the ten years of unfettered immunity and lack of bloodshed between us, which I have been so graciously offered by our human companions this evening," he gestured to Dani, "can be yours."

He paused, now standing directly in front of the pulpit.

"Now, I believe you have a choice to make gentleman. I'll leave you for a moment to discuss." He nodded, eyes flashing crimson, before he swiftly took his leave. "Choose wisely."

10

T he moment Corbin finished his speech, Dani tore from the room, more thankful than ever for the reprieve. She hadn't been able to breathe since the moment Cassandra had walked in, moving with all the grace of a preternatural beast. A kind of grace to which she could never aspire. Not if Corbin had his say.

She found her refuge in the choir room, her heart still racing. She could hardly keep her balance, hardly think.

Why was it so difficult to breathe? Though, if she was honest, she already knew.

Because Corbin had an entire life, an entire existence before her. Hell, likely several, and yet, he'd never bothered to share it with her. It was one more sign of how little importance she was to him. One more reason she needed to take fate into her own hands.

Dani's mind wandered, each recollection of Cassandra's words bringing fresh pain again.

Suddenly, Dani felt as if she'd been transported then, back to several years earlier as she stood outside another mansion, another party, one that was so much like the one she'd attended with him two nights before. An unexpected rain as she'd walked up the driveaway, her taxi driver unable to navigate through the sea of town cards and private limousines, had left her soaked through, ruining her dress and smearing her makeup, until she was certain she'd looked awful, but none of that had mattered, or it at least, it wasn't supposed to, as she'd stood on the steps, waiting outside the entrance to the party for longer than she knew.

She'd waited, and waited, and waited, until still he hadn't come.

And finally, when others noticed she was waiting too, for the first time in her life she'd felt like a fool. For assuming Corbin could ever want her, for mistaking his kindness as an invite to be his mistress, or at the very least, the woman on his arm for the night.

She'd been about to go home. She even would have walked if she had to. Anything was better than standing there, realizing she'd been made a fool. She turned to leave then, only for Cillian to stop her by her wrist.

"Come inside," he'd whispered, his voice a glamour filled hiss. "Come inside and join me, Dani."

Abruptly, the door to the choir room opened, startling Dani from the memory. The door shut just as quickly, sealing behind whoever entered.

Dani swiped at the tears which prickled at the corner of her eyes and spun to face him. "You could have told me that you—"

She stopped; her words cut short.

"You thought I was Corbin, didn't you?" Cassandra asked, taking a step toward her. "Don't worry. He's looking for you. I just happened to get to you first."

Dani stepped back a little, placing more distance between them. "Please, don't hurt me."

At that, Cassandra threw back her head and laughed, her joy a sharp, and shrill cackle. "Now, explain to me why I would want to do that, hmmm?" She trailed her manicured fingers over a nearby music stand, her words sharper than its metal edges. "Corbin already wants me dead for how I sold him out to Lucien. Touching you would make me a fool."

There was that word again, the one she'd used to disparage herself. Dani didn't know how Cassandra knew the power it held over her, but the siren latched onto it like a hungry babe at the tit.

"You make him look foolish, you know? Every time he stands beside you when he could be standing by me." Cassandra ran both hands over her breasts, down the curves of her sides, curves any woman would have envied. "I'm more beautiful than you'll ever be," she whispered through pouty, full lips. "Anyone with eyes can see it."

"You're right," Dani admitted. "You *are* beautiful." She let her gaze fall over Cassandra's form, appreciating. "Flawless really."

Cassandra preened, smiling that smug grin of hers.

"But Corbin sees my flaws, scars and all," Dani gestured to her own body, "and he likes those, too." She met Cassandra's eyes then. "I don't think he'd say the same for you." Forcing herself to be braver than she usually would be— practice, she supposed—Dani stepped forward. "You may be beautiful, Cassandra. More beautiful and powerful than I'll ever be."

Her gaze raked over the other woman, voice lowering to a whisper. "But inside you're ugly, and it's what a man thinks when he's *inside* that really counts." Dani drew toe-to-painted-toe with the other woman, turning down her nose at her. "You'd best run back to Angelo. No doubt he'll be missing you."

"Don't be surprised when he gets bored with you," Cassandra said, a surprising flash of pain in her eyes. "Corbin took longer than most, but eventually, they all grow bored with you." To Dani's surprise, Cassandra left without another word, slithering back to her new lover. Thankfully for Dani's pride, the gorgeous siren had miscalculated on exactly where to hit Dani to make it hurt, what to say truly undo her. It wasn't Cassandra's beauty Dani envied. Dani was a beauty in her own right. True: a human beauty, but a beauty, nonetheless.

No, it wasn't Cassandra's sumptuous looks that drew Dani in, made her heart turn green with envy. It was the power Cassandra exuded from every pore. The power that came from being a siren, from being an untouchable, super-natural entity. Someone who could defend herself, who didn't have to rely on anyone to save her anymore.

And given time, if Dani had her say, she'd claim that same power for herself.

And her revenge against Lucien, too.

It was all within her grasp. All she needed to do was reach out and take it.

CORBIN HAD SCOURED the whole of the church's interior and had even contemplated clomping across the grounds all the way to the rectory, before finally on his second pass through the main corridor, Cassandra blew past him, spitting angry. "She's in the choir room, if you must keep searching."

Corbin quickened his steps, moving a faster. Reaching

the choir room shortly, he paused momentarily, before finally charging in.

Dani sat in one of the practice chairs, her back facing toward him, staring up at a painted portrait of Christ, as she thumbed through an abandoned music sheet.

"Is it true?" she whispered, not bothering to turn toward him. "Tell me, is it true?"

"Whatever Cassandra said to you Dani, it—"

"Is it true that you grew bored of Cassandra and that's why you left her? From my guess, only a handful of days before me."

Corbin chose his next words carefully. "I've lived a very long life, Dani. I won't apologize for having relationships before you."

"I don't expect you too," she whispered softly, her voice cracking a little. "But why didn't you tell me you had a wife? Children too?"

The question settled between them, unsurprisingly heavy.

"I lost them a very long time ago," Corbin said, treading gently. "I don't see why it's—"

"Because it's important to you," Dani snapped, glancing over her shoulder toward him. There were tears running down her face, fat, wet tears, tears full of real emotion, something he'd once worried he hadn't felt in decades. Not until Dani at least. "They were important to you, so they're important to me," she whispered, instinctively knowing the kindest thing she could say. "Tell me about them."

Corbin stood silent for a long time, searching for the right words to say, and realizing there were no words that would ever do them justice. They were thoughts, feelings. Memories lost in the sands of time, slowly drifting away with each passing day.

And still, their loss haunted him.

"Rosalind would have loved you," he said finally, speaking of her for the first time in an age. "She was a kind and gentle woman, a survivor, much like you. Fearsome only when she needed to be. Plague had taken most of her siblings very young, so she wanted a large family. Most women at that time did. She always longed for a sister. She was, in truth, a woman set in her ways—quiet, full of virtue —but I think, despite your differences, she would have adored you."

"And your children?"

Corbin hesitated. "It's still too difficult to speak of them, but we...we lost them, shortly after Rosalind faded away. Elias and Gertrude. Elias lived to the old age of twenty and three, only to be lost to smallpox. Gertrude barely made it to two."

"I'm sorry."

"When Rosalind died, they were lost without their mother. They relied on her, as children are ought to do. Sometimes, I think...sometimes I think if she hadn't died so soon after I... after I was changed, that they would have lived, too. That I would have been able to see them through."

"You can't possibly know that, Corbin. You can't blame your—"

"I can," he said, not allowing a moment of her pity. "I can and will continue to blame myself, because their deaths were mine too."

Dani lifted a brow, clearly misunderstanding.

"Shortly after I was turned, I...I tried to turn Rosalind."

The sharp hiss of Dani's breath told him she knew. She knew what a poor choice that'd been, though at the time *he* hadn't. "Newly turned vampires have little control, you see," his voice continued, though it felt as if it'd been, disembodied from him. "They're not yet fit to become sires. Had I known...had my own sire ensured I was properly educated then, maybe..."

"Oh, Corbin." Dani stood, making her way toward him.

"I do not want nor need your pity." He shook his head, refusing to accept her outstretched hand.

Slowly, it returned to her side once more.

"I only ask that you try to understand, why I—"

"Why you refuse to turn me," she finished for him. "Why you're afraid."

"It's not turning you I'm afraid of, Dani," he said, finally holding her stare. "It's the risk of losing you, that thing that makes you *you*. It's not something I can do."

Dani was shaking her head, refusing to see his reasoning. "But Corbin, if you don't turn me, you'll still lose me. I'll grow old. I'll rot away and turn into—"

"But first you will have lived," he countered. "First, you will have lived a long and happy life, far away from this world. *That* is what I hope for you."

"And what about what I hope for, too?" Dani patted a hand against her chest, indicating the heart that beat beneath. "Have you ever stopped to consider what *I* hope for too?" She shook her head at him, incredulously. "All my life I've been preyed upon, hurt, by men like you."

Corbin bristled at the insinuation, but still she continued.

"I can no longer find a home among humanity when I'm the only human in every room who knows about you, your world, about all the dark and twisted and beautiful things that wait just beyond the dark. That kind of knowledge, when you bear it alone, it kills you softly, sweetly, Corbin."

"Dani—"

She held up a hand, causing him to fall silent once more. "I'm not yet finished," she said, inhaling a breath clearly meant to fortify herself. "I know your world. I know the human one too. I've seen the darkness in both and been given a chance to choose, and while I'm certain my brother will hate me for it, it's *your* world I choose. The world I know best. The world without rules. The world that, if you turn me, will empower me in ways I've never known, because I will be born anew, and most importantly, I will be able to share in that newfound power with you." She met his eyes then, her irises once again teeming with tears. "I've loved you for years, Corbin, even when you have not loved me."

The silence that stretched between them then felt vaster than eternity.

"Please say something," Dani whispered.

Corbin shook his head, sitting down on one of the nearby choir chairs, before he ran both his hands through his hair. "You know nothing of what you speak," he said, refusing to look at her.

Dani bristled. "I have lived in your world for more than—"

"That's not what I mean, Dani," he snapped. "Do not ever claim that I—"

"You left me there, Corbin," she hurled the words at him, tears falling violently. "You left me standing alone at that godforsaken party. Or was it so insignificant to you that you can't even be bothered to remem—"

"I did it to protect you!" he shouted, standing once more. "I did it to protect you, because I have loved you since the moment I first held you in my arms years ago. And I will continue to protect you, from this too. As I've done countless times before. As I *continue* to do, even in my weakest moments." He dropped his gaze to her lips, brushing the spot where he'd first smeared her lipstick. "Even when I almost came back to you."

Corbin could see the exact moment Dani's breath caught. Could hear the way her heart raced as he reached just above her breasts, pulling the delicate gold chain which laid against her skin, until the skeleton key appeared. "You never once questioned who gave this to you. Who would leave you such a message?"

Dani shivered a little, practically vibrating with untold emotion. "I...I didn't think—"

"No, you didn't." He released the key, allowing it to fall round her neck once more. "You didn't once think that denying you, leaving you, could possibly hurt me too."

She was crying again. Tears aplenty. "I didn't know."

"Of course," he cupped her chin in his hand. "How could you? How could you when I worked to hide it so well?" His hand slipped around the back of her neck, pulling her to him.

He claimed her lips then, pouring every emotion he felt into it, no matter how new. Every joy, every heartache, every misguided quest for revenge. He gifted it all too her. Everything he'd once held back. Everything he'd thought he could feel no more. Save for one final confession.

By the time Corbin broke the kiss between them, they were both panting, Corbin's cock growing hard as the claimed one another in a delicious battle of tongue, touch, and teeth.

But he wouldn't be dissuaded from gifting his truth to her. Not this time.

"Do you know what this is a key to?" he asked, once more clutching the chain of the necklace. "This is a key to my heart, to my home. That's why I gave it you to."

Dani looked a little confused, causing him to smile. "To

your penthouse?" she asked, as if the answer were a little anticlimactic.

Corbin chuckled. "Yes and no," he said, drawing her to him once more. "You'll find it works there these days, but it was originally designed for a small cabin in Yorkshire. A home that belonged to my parents." He cleared his throat. "To me and my wife, too, before she died." Saying these things was far harder than he'd anticipated, but he hadn't come this far only to run at the first sign of fear. "She would have wanted it to belong to you." He kissed her, a soft brush, gentle brush of lips. "To someone who brings me more happiness than I have any right to."

"Then turn me, Corbin," she pleaded. "Why won't you allow me that same happiness, too?" She smoothed a single hand over his cheek. "An eternity of it?"

"Because I cannot do that to you, Dani. I cannot bear the thought of your death being on my hands, bear the memory of you dying in my arms. It's why I left you standing in the rain on Cillian's porch that evening, why I threw myself over you in that ballroom, even though I thought I might still lose you, even though I knew I might lose my revenge against Lucien, too. And I'd do it all again. I'd do it all again in an instant."

"Your revenge?" Dani's eyes suddenly grew wide. "Lucien," she breathed, a knowing gleam passing through her eyes. "Lucien is the vampire who sired you, only to abandon you," she said, finally making the connection.

"Yes." Corbin didn't say anything further on the matter.

He didn't have to.

"Which means...your wife, your children wouldn't have died had Lucien not turned you, not left you unknowing of your own kind's ways, your own weaknesses, and yet, I...I took your chance away from you. Your revenge." Her voice trailed off.

Dani gripped him by his shirt then, suddenly desperate. "What can I do? What can I do to make it right?"

"There's nothing you can do, darling, short of saving yourself." He wiped one of her tears away with his thumb, where it trailed across her cheek. "I'm a broken man, Dani. No one can undo that. Not even you. So, when this is through, leave. Leave this world and never come back."

"I can't." She shook her head, pulling away from him. "I can't do that to you."

"You can and you will, Dani." He captured her in his arms. Dani. His love. His fearsome huntress. A sharp-eyed harpy disguised as an angel. "Go forth, darling. *Live* your life. Live it well and full of joy as I know you can do. Find a husband, a *human* husband, one who will laugh and cry and have children with you, beautiful blue-eyed children that will make your belly and heart so full, you'll never once long for the things you left behind you."

"I don't want that," she cried. "Don't you see? I don't want any of that, unless it's with you."

"I can't give you that life, Dani. I cannot give you any kind of life at all. I can only give you death."

A slow clap sounded behind them, as sharp as it was sarcastic. "This has all been rather touching, truly, but there's someone waiting for you." Cassandra scowled, before beckoning them back into the main room.

Corbin wasn't the least bit surprised by the new faces he found waiting there.

"Lucien," he said.

"Quinn," Dani echoed, as if it were a chore for her to breathe. She came to stand beside him then, staring at her brother, shaking her head a little, as if for the first time ever he'd disappointed her too. "What did you do?" she breathed, eyes darting toward Lucien momentarily.

"I warned you, Dani," Quinn said, slipping off his Stetson and placing it over his heart as if in apology. "I warned you there was a split in the organization."

Corbin didn't need to hear the steady beat of Dani's heart to know it'd been ripped in two, decimated by a man who had the gall to consider himself her family. "So, you decided to throw your lot in with the vampire who raped me and come for my boyfriend, too?" She gaped at him.

"To be clear," Corbin said, in an attempt to lighten the mood, "I am too old to be called anyone's boyfriend, darling. Only lover will do," he said, glaring directly at Quinn.

Apparently, he was now taking his cues from Cassandra and Angelo when it came to pettiness. But in this case, he'd take whatever shot he could take.

"There was nothing I could do." Quinn swallowed. His apology appeared sincere. "I'm sorry, Dani."

"And I suppose it's the same for you?" Corbin asked, turning to address the other members of the bloodsucking crowd. "You'd all continue to war amongst yourselves sooner than bow to another?"

Angelo shrugged. "It's politics. Nothing personal, Corbin. But between me and you, it'll always be me I choose." He stroked a hand down Cassandra's leg. "And Sandy, of course."

Sandy? Corbin lifted a brow toward Cassandra as if to say, *You sell me out and this is the idiot you go running to?*

Cassandra shrugged her expression implying, *He's better than you.*

At least that was one area in which they were in agreement, because while the other vampires in the room were just as ancient, and lethal as he was, *he* was the snake in the

Garden, the one precious Eve had been tempted to, and for a man who'd crafted his life as if it were a stage, his last act was hardly through.

"Of course," Corbin said, his smile twisting into something fierce. "Which is why I planned for your betrayal. All of you." His eyes turned toward Quinn and Lucien, then to the other bosses of the syndicate. "Consider this fleeting moment my goodbye gift to you."

11

Corbin's signal to his men didn't make the hit any less sudden.

The sound of gunfire was never really something one got used to, or at least Corbin hadn't, in all his many years. It rattled in his eardrums, ricocheting off the walls as he dropped to the ground beside Dani, dragging her to the ground with him, exactly as they'd planned to do, with some help from Kharis, too. They'd agreed the combination of their individual tactics would be the best move, helping them *both* claim a swift and fierce revenge.

One their enemies would no doubt whisper about for years to come.

The first round passed rather quickly, leaving the floor teeming in blood and bullets. The shattered shards of the stained-glass windows sparkling like jewels.

Slowly, Corbin staggered to his feet. To his surprise, Angelo was the first to move, twitching awake from where he and Cassandra had clutched each other. The other vampire rushed him, meaty fists heaving, but Corbin was ready for him. He fired a shot point-blank, his aim straight into Angelo's forehead. The other vampire dropped to the ground like a fool.

Corbin would leave his men to finish Angelo for good later.

Mickey came next, his strike swift and sure, his blade cutting across Corbin's cheek. But Corbin relieved him of his weapon swiftly. Mickey may have been fast on his feet, but Corbin was far older, far more powerful. He gutted the bastard.

Thankfully, for now, the others stayed down, which meant, he'd deal with them later. Swiping the blood Mickey had drawn from his cheek, he climbed the stairs of the altar, retrieving the wooden crucifix Dani had pointed him to. He broke the end of it over one knee, splintering it in two. It wasn't exactly as a sharp of a stake as he would have liked, but it would have to do.

He made his way over to where Lucien lay then, gurgling as the blood beneath him pooled. He was helpless and vulnerable, as Corbin had once been when Lucien had attacked him, changed him.

"Contrary to what one would think, I'm not one to stand on ceremony, so I won't ask if you have any last words," he said, raising the stake in his hands. "You wouldn't deserve such an utterance anyway, but here are mine and Dani's last words delivered to you." He leaned down, drawing so close that only Lucien could hear.

"I hope the devil shoves a blinding hot poker up your arse every day from now until the end of time itself," he hissed. "Oh, and we can't forget Dani's contribution, can we?" Corbin smiled devilishly. "She told me to simply to stab you through your bleeding, undead heart with a cold and rousing fuck you." Corbin raised the stake over Lucien's chest. "So, cheers to that, old boy."

Corbin plunged the broken crucifix down into Lucien's chest, ending the other vampire in an instant. Blood spray spattered over him, coating him from head to toe, practically bathing him in it. He had half a mind to wear it like a badge of honor, at least until he made love to Dani later in the day.

Dani, who was supposed to be standing at his side, watching him see their plan through.

Corbin rose to his feet, wiping the blood from his eyes with the back of his hand, though it was equally soaked. "Well, I'd say you all played your roles rather well, especially you—" He turned to where Dani should have stood, to where Kharis and Quinn, and the others who'd agreed to join his ruse had started to rise.

But Dani was still lying on the floor, her chest hardly moving.

"Dani?" he said, taking a tentative step toward her. "Dani!"

True fear raced through him.

Suddenly, Corbin was at her side, not even having felt himself move.

He ripped the bulk of the coat she wore away, the one meant to hide the bulletproof vest she'd been supposed to wear beneath, but there was no vest there. In its place, there were nothing but blood. Her sweet, sweet blood, and the thin material of her dress.

Corbin was shaking, barely capable of forming words, as he clutched hold of her face, tapping at her cheek to rouse her awake.

Dani let out a pained groan, her eyes fluttering open to stare up at the cathedral ceiling.

"Why didn't you wear your vest, darling? Why didn't you wear the vest I gave you?"

Dani let out a shuddering breath, as if speaking had

suddenly become a chore she didn't care for. "You told me to leave," she rasped. "You told me to leave and I...I couldn't do this without you. I...won't be anyone's plaything, Corbin. I won't allow others to make my decisions for me. Not even you, so, I...took a risk, made a choice."

"And so, you chose *this*, instead?" Corbin shouted his fury.

At her or at the heavens, the fates, he didn't know who.

He didn't know fucking anything anymore. Up or down. Left or right. Right or wrong.

None of it made any fucking sense. Not if he was going to lose her.

Just after they'd finally found each other.

No. No, he couldn't lose her, goddamnit. Not like this.

Slowly, Dani's face twisted toward him. "It's what you wanted, didn't you? For me to," she sputtered, coughing up blood, "l-live a full life? To die before you? Of...of natural causes."

"There's nothing natural about my men putting a bullet in you!" he cried. "Goddamn it, woman!" Sweat gathered on his forehead, beading there, now that fear ruled him.

He couldn't lose her. Not like this. Not like this.

"I'm sorry," she whispered, trying and failing to touch his cheek. "I...I need to ask you to save me one time more."

One time more.

As if before she'd even come here, she'd somehow already known everything he'd held back from her before. About Rosalind. Elias. Gertrude. Even about the skeleton key. About how he'd tried to protect her from the worst parts of himself, only for that singular decision to place her in more and more trouble along the way. He could fall on his knees before her, grovel for the rest of his years, and still, it wouldn't be enough. *He* wouldn't be enough.

Which was exactly why he'd left her.

Though she'd never resorted to anything this drastic.

Never alone anyway. And now, he was going to lose her.

Corbin's eyes combed the room, searching and finding his target. "You," he snarled at Kharis, voice trembling. "You did this, didn't you?"

Kharis shrugged, like he failed to see how it mattered. "I might have helped her a little along the way."

Corbin snarled, baring his fangs.

"Self-sacrificial doesn't suit you. We needed something to snap you out of it."

"And so, you thought it might be a good idea to *kill* the woman I love?" Corbin roared his fury, standing and pacing beside where Dani now lay at his feet. He gripped at his scalp, fisting his hair so hard his knuckles turned white. "Fix this," he demanded, pointing toward her, to where she was barely breathing. "Fix this, Kharis. Hell, turn her if you must."

"Do you really want her to be mine that way?" Kharis said, his expression unmoving. "Are you truly so afraid of losing her that you would hand her away for forever? To *me* of all people?"

Like all vampires, Kharis had more than a little darkness of his own. They all ended up that way, twisted, corrupted over the years.

"Corbin," Dani rasped, blood gurgling out of her mouth, reaching up in search for him.

Corbin fell to her side again, hands clammy and shaking. "I'm here, darling. I'm here." He gripped her hand, brushing a stray strand of hair from her face.

"I'm...cold," she whispered. "So cold."

For the first time in a century Corbin felt his emotions catch inside his throat. "I know, darling. I know. It'll end soon enough." Corbin shut his eyes then, surprised to find himself crying. He hadn't even known he was capable of it anymore.

"Turn her, Corbin," Kharis said, from where he stood beside them. "If you love her, turn her. Then maybe this tragedy can become a celebration another day."

Corbin was shaking, struggling to fight his own fear. "I love you, darling. Now and until we both shall meet again in the next life," he whispered, his words almost feverish.

"It's what she wants, what she demands of you," Kharis continued. "It's what Rosalind wanted, too, but what you were too young to see then is that it was as much her choice as it was yours. It's the same for Dani. She made her choice, and she chose you."

Kharis crouched down, holding Dani's head so that her neck tilted toward Corbin. The last fluttering beats of her pulse almost at a close. "So, drink now, brother. You're stronger than you were before. Drink now and drink deep."

And with one final, striking bite Corbin took his fill, until he felt Dani slip away in his arms.

EPILOGUE

Twenty years later...

"You're late," Dani said, staring down the steps from where she stood outside their glittering mansion home, pointing to the watch she kept inside her purse pocket. "You promised you'd be on time."

"I'd never purposefully be late to meet you, darling," Corbin said, as she gave him a disbelieving look. "Well, not any longer, anyway," he smirked, quickly trying to appease her with kisses. First on her ear, then her chin, then the soft skin of her neck where her pulse thumped away.

It was slower now. It's beat inhuman, but he wouldn't have it any other way.

Not anymore.

"How someone can be late to their own party, I'll never know." She turned, wrapping her arms around his neck as she sighed against him. "But somehow, you manage it every year."

"These things are as much for you as they are for me, darling. It may be my speeches they come to hear, but it's your work that gives the true advantage."

Somehow, it'd only taken her a handful of years to convince him that his talents, which had made him so successful in the syndicate, would be better spent on nonprofits, helping the charities that were the most desperate for funds. This year, the organization had been of her choosing, one to benefit victims of sexual violence.

Becoming a vampire hadn't stopped the nightmares which still sometimes plagued her, but it had lessened them over the years, as Dani slowly came into the full of her power.

She no longer needed him to save her.

In fact, he was certain it'd been her that'd truly been saving *him* for years.

Pulling him back from the darkest parts of himself whenever he risked going over the edge. Like when he'd allowed his fear to dictate his love for her.

The whole thing seemed foolish now, now that he no longer feared losing her.

What was there to fear when they had the whole of time ahead of them?

"What are you thinking?" Dani whispered, her fangs nipping and nicking against his ear.

He growled his approval. "I was thinking we could skip this whole thing, go straight to bed, and not leave there for years."

"Mmm," she hummed her approval. "Sounds tempting." She trailed a hand down his arm, stepping back a little, her signature move, meant to tempt him, to make him remember on nights like this. "But first you owe me a dance." She sauntered away from him then, swaying her hips a bit as she had on so many nights like this before.

It was a reminder of where they'd come from, where they'd once been.

And that, for better or worse, they still had an eternity in store, together.

ABOUT THE AUTHOR

Kait Ballenger is the award-winning author of the Seven Range Shifter and Rogue Brotherhood paranormal romance series, where she weaves captivating tales filled with dark, sexy alpha heroes and the independent women who bring them to their knees.

When Kait's not preoccupied writing "intense and riveting" paranormal plots or "high-voltage" love scenes that make even seasoned romance readers blush, she can usually be found spending time with her family or with her nose buried in a good book. She lives in Florida with her husband and two sons.

Readers can visit Kait's website and sign up for her newsletter at www.kaitballenger.com.

For right inquiries, contact Nicole Resciniti at The Seymour Agency: nicole@theseymouragency.com

ACKNOWLEDGMENTS

First and foremost thanks go to the ladies of the HEA Collective. Without you, this story simply would not be. Thank you for including me among such a fabulous group of authors.

To my friend, Mara Wells, for the proofread. I will always appreciate your friendship.

And finally, to my husband, Jon, for the brainstorming and the endless Godfather references.

ALSO BY KAIT BALLENGER

Seven Range Shifters

Cowboy Wolf Trouble

Cowboy in Wolf's Clothing

Wicked Cowboy Wolf

Fierce Cowboy Wolf

Wild Cowboy Wolf

Cowboy Wolf Outlaw

Cowboy Wolf Christmas

The Rogue Brotherhood

Shadow Hunter

Rogue Wolf Hunter